Necronado
RJ Roles

Contents

Dedication	V
Based on a true story...	1
...kinda.	3
Prologue	5
Chapter One	15
Chapter Two	29
Chapter Three	43
Chapter Four	63
Chapter Five	75
Chapter Six	87
Chapter Seven	109
Chapter Eight	125
Chapter Nine	145
Chapter Ten	165
Chapter Eleven	173
Chapter Twelve	191
Chapter Thirteen	201
Epilogue	213

About the Author 219

Also By RJ Roles 221

Copyrights 222

First and foremost, this book is dedicated to Justin Woodward, without whom the idea behind this book would not exist. Second, to Mike Ennenbach, who pushed me to keep going with it, encouraging me along the way until I finally drove the final nail into the coffin. To my wife, Jessica, who always has my back no matter what. To Marcie Robinson and Dominic Lagonigro, who are always there to read whatever craziness I have conjured and offer feedback. And to so many more that keep me uplifted and in the right headspace, even in the darkest of times. You all know who you are. And as always, to you, dear reader, without whom these words are just floating in the ether, without purpose or meaning.

Based on a true story...

...kinda.

Prologue

J erry was doing his best not to turn around and murder his girlfriend with the flashlight he was holding. Her nagging had started long before they left his '93 Chevy Cavalier on the side of the road and started their trek up to the old Foster Farm family cemetery.

"How much farther, Jerry? All this grass is making my legs itch," Anna complained.

Jerry stopped dead in his tracks and turned to look at Anna's pale, moonlit face. "How many times do I gotta tell you not to call me Jerry? I go by 'Bones' now, goddamnit," he said, holding the bag he was toting out in front of him, air-thrusting into it a few times.

"Sorry, I just thought that was for when we were around the other guys," she replied. "You'll always be my little 'Jerrbear', though." Anna pouted her lips and gazed at him with puppy dog eyes.

Jerry rolled his eyes before turning away, heading for the cemetery. He'd always hated that nickname, but had endured it since Anna was hot as hell and had taken his v-card one night out at Quarry Lake. They both had had too much to drink, and the next morning, Jerry woke up with nothing but a shirt on—a true Winnie the Pooh moment—with Anna halfway draped over him. He couldn't remember anything that happened, but when he looked down and saw her ample tits pressed against him, it was lust at first sight.

Now, here they were, five months later, and he'd finally been able to talk her into doing this gnarly ritual he'd read about on the internet.

"I told you where we'd be going tonight. You shoulda wore pants," he said, shifting the bag on his shoulder as he blazed their path.

"Yeah, but I didn't think we'd be walking this far through a damn jungle. Plus, I wanted to look cute for you."

Jerry stopped and looked back again, shining a flashlight to see her wiggling her ass at him in her booty shorts. "You ain't cute, babe. You're sexy as fuck."

Anna beamed at Jerry as she looked over her shoulder, giving him one final wiggle in appreciation.

"I think it's just on top of this hill, if I remember right. Then the fun really begins," he said with a laugh.

As he crested the hill, the light from the full moon lit the tops of old, weathered tombstones that poked up out of patches of tall weeds. Some were toppled and laying on the ground, while others were crumbling where they stood, defiant against all that nature could throw at them. Aiming the flashlight at the nearest one, the inscription was hard to make out, but he thought the date was from the 1800s.

"Bitchin'," Anna said as she reached the cemetery.

Jerry didn't answer vocally, but he nodded in agreement, a wide grin spreading across his face. Anna grabbed the flashlight from his hand and started pointing it at different grave markers.

"Holy shit, these things are old as shit. There are at least fifteen or so dating back to over a hundred years ago."

"Yeah, I know. Bring that light over here," Jerry said as he dropped the bag off his shoulder to the ground and started looking through it. "Babe?" He looked up to see what was taking her so long and saw Anna standing over one of the smaller markers. "Baaabe?"

"Coming," she said, lost in thought.

Jerry pulled an old, soiled blanket from the bag that they kept in his car for when they felt adventurous and wanted to have sex in the woods. Next came a battered Ouija board.

"Where did that thing come from?" Anna asked, giving it a side-eyed glance.

Jerry looked up and grinned—the moonlight giving his face a sinister aura. "Found it at Goodwill for like three bucks. Pretty fuckin' sweet, right?"

"Yeah, I guess..."

"Hey, hold that light steady."

As Jerry pulled out four candles and placed them on the blanket, Anna scoffed and bent down to inspect them.

"Are these my good candles from the bathroom?"

Looking up, blank-faced, Jerry said, "Uh, yeah," and rolled his eyes.

"Un-fucking-real."

"Would you just chill?" he said and he upended the bag, spilling the rest of its contents onto the blanket.

"And that? What do you need a knife for?" Anna asked, wrapping her arms around herself as a gust of wind blew over the hilltop.

Jerry sighed. "Jesus Christ, Anna. Have you never seen a horror movie before? If you want to perform a ritualistic summoning, you need some basic tools. And a badass dagger is one of them."

After spreading out the blanket on the ground, Jerry arranged everything he'd brought, using the Ouija board as the centerpiece.

"Now what, Jer— *Bones*?" Anna asked.

Looking around at the headstones, then shifting to his set-up, Jerry bit his lip, trying to remember. "Oh!" he remembered, reaching into his pocket, pulling out a folded piece of paper.

The moon had reached its pinnacle, making it easier to read the instructions he'd printed off without the aid of the flashlight. He loved that it even had step-by-step pictures.

"Says we should light the candles."

Jerry retrieved a Zippo from his pocket and rolled the wheel several times before a flame sparked to life. He motioned for Anna to join him on the blanket after the candles were lit.

"Now... we gotta say these words together."

"What language is that? And what does it mean?" Anna asked, squinting at the text.

Jerry shrugged. "Shit if I know, but that's the next step."

Together, they sounded out what was written on the instructions as best they could.

"Te invoco a profundus inferni!"

Anna looked around, her hair swooshing as she did. "Nothing happened," she said.

Jerry sat silent for a moment, a deep frown forming on his face. He pulled the instruction up close to read over them. "Ah, we need to use the dagger."

"What the hell does it mean by 'use' it?" Anna asked, her face becoming a mixture of perplexity and concern.

"Says we need to cut our palms and join them together while we recite the words." Jerry picked up the dagger and grabbed Anna's hand.

"Nah, uh, Jerry. Fuck you. You are not cutting me with that thing." She quickly jerked her hand away from him.

"Come on, babe. We're almost done. This has been so awesome. Don't you want to finish up to see what happens?"

A laugh escaped out of her mouth as she thought of the countless times Jerry left her to "finish up" after he passed out. "Fine. But it better be a small cut. And I want you to take me to get my nails done in the morning."

"Deal!" he agreed, visibly grateful she was willing.

The dagger was dull and it took Jerry several attempts before he was able to pierce Anna's skin—her wincing the whole time.

"Fuck, did you really have to dig around like that?" she asked, staring at the wound as it wept blood.

Ignoring her question, Jerry's tongue stuck out the side of his mouth as he worked the dagger into his own palm. "There," he said, showing her his own ragged, torn flesh.

When they coupled their hands together, their bonded blood seeped through their interlocked fingers as they said the words again.

"Fuck! Why isn't anything happening?" Jerry yelled in frustration.

"May I?" Anna asked, holding out her free hand for the instructions. They kept their hands locked as she read; Jerry sulked.

"Well?"

"Well... you almost had it right," she replied. "But you're supposed to stab the blood coated dagger into the Ouija board while we... chant the weird phrases, over and over. After that, it says you will find yourself irresistible to anyone you find attractive. Jerry, what the fuck? Are you dumping me?" Anna asked in a shrill voice.

"Of course not, babe. Why would I? You are *so* fucking fine." Jerry thought he recovered well and sounded convincing enough. "I just thought... you know, what if we're at a show or something and you spot a pretty young thing you want to take home and play with?"

Anna gave him the side-eye while biting her lip. "Fine. But only ones that I pick."

Jerry grinned. "Of course."

Taking the dagger, he slid it in between their hands, getting a nice, thick layer of blood on the blade. A forceful gust of wind blew over the cemetery as they began to chant.

"Te invoco a profundus inferni!"

Every time they repeated the chant, their voices grew louder to combat the growing gusts. The chant became their mantra, taking over and becoming the couple's sole purpose for living. The clouds above raced across the sky, but they were too hyper-focused on the chant to notice. Raising the dagger high above his head, the wind whipped around Jerry—splashing droplets of blood across nearby tombstones—before he plunged it into the Ouija board.

Thunder clapped when the blade made contact with the spirit board. Anna flinched and looked skyward, seeing the brewing storm overhead. When she looked down at Jerry, his eyes had rolled back, leaving only the white sclera showing. His mouth was still moving, still repeating the strange words.

"Jerr-bear, I don't like this. Please make it stop."

Anna tried to free her hand from his, but Jerry's hand held her in a vice-like grip. Even shaking and pulling on him couldn't break him out of the trance he was in. His recitement quickened, matching the wind that seemed to be coming from all directions.

"Hey, cut it the fuck out," she screamed.

A bolt of lightning streaked down from the sky, striking one of the tallest and oldest headstones that was topped with a heavily weathered crucifix. Anna shrieked with surprise. More bolts struck around the cemetery, and when she looked up, Anna saw a swirling vortex forming directly above them. In her mind, Anna thought it looked like the tumultuous sky was unfurling a finger in the form of a hellacious funnel.

She felt Jerry's grip slacken, then finally released her hand. When she tore her eyes away from the descending twister and looked, he now had his arms held up, as if in some kind of mock praise.

"We need to get the fuck out of here, Jerry! Right now!"

Anna rose to her feet, grabbed Jerry's arm, and tried to pull him up. He stayed planted to the spot—his eyes still rolled back and the strange words spilling out of his mouth.

The wind was howling at a fever pitch as it blew through the cemetery. Smaller bits of debris were being tossed around, and the lightning strikes were getting worse.

Anna's attention was drawn to the path they had blazed to get to the cemetery, when a sound like nothing she'd ever heard in her life groaned then cracked like a whip. The cyclone had touched down to the ground and was chewing up anything and everything in its path.

Trying one last time, she pleaded to Jerry, "Get the fuck up or we're going to fucking die!" Even though she was screaming, her words were barely audible over the noise pollution of the storm.

Anna saw the twister was headed straight for them. "Fuck you, Jerry. You suck!"

The clouds opened up, water and debris were now raining havoc down on the long-forgotten cemetery.

When Anna turned to run, she tripped over a fallen headstone and her eyes grew wide when she saw how close the twister was. She felt its suction and crawled as fast as she could to one of the bigger monuments.

The funnel tore through the cemetery with ease, pulling up tombstones as if they were dandelions. What shocked her the most was when she saw the first set of bones being ripped from the ground.

Watching in horror as the ritual-induced tornado shucked the interred from their final resting places, Anna grabbed ahold of the aged stone and held on—white-knuckled and scared senseless.

She watched as, one by one, all the grave markers fell like dominos—along with a flurry of bones—to the wrath of the twister. During all the turmoil, Jerry stayed in the same spot he'd been in from the start—arms still raised.

When the pulling force of the wind increased, Anna felt her legs being lifted off the ground, followed by her body. Her grip on the monument was the only thing keeping her from flying into the heart of the savage tornado.

Even though she was fighting to maintain her grip, Anna saw how unaffected Jerry seemed to be by the storm. Her boyfriend was in the direct path of the twister, but she thought it was slowing down in its approach. From her perspective, it looked as though he was worshiping the damn thing.

And then...

...it started to consume him. First by stripping the flesh away from his outstretched arms, then shredding away his clothes and skin beneath. Bit by bit, pieces of Jerry were torn away until only his praising skeleton was left kneeling in reverence to the tornado's might. And then his bones were sucked into the cyclone of death.

Anna's dread was palpable, and she didn't know how much longer her hands could hold on.

As her legs wavered in the air like streamers on a set of handlebars, her thoughts turned back to Jerry—at least for a moment. *I'm so going to kick your ass for this, Jerr-bear!*

One finger, then two, then a hand lost its hold. Anna looked up in terror as the fingers on her other hand started to peel away. With only two still clinging to the stone, she let out a whimper just before they released.

Unseen by the naked eye, the tornado was spinning so fast, the debris it had picked up created its own sub-vortex on the outside. Similar to a wood chipper, Anna was sliced, diced, and ultimately misted into a fine spray in an instant when she was sucked in, joining Jerry and the other residents of the Foster Farm family cemetery.

Howling with unadulterated savagery, the twister turned its wrath toward the sleepy town of Lordsland in the distance.

Chapter One

Jake Ward stepped onto the back deck of his house and surveyed the land. He'd just seen his wife and son off—kissing them both goodbye—and wanted to check out any damages that may have occurred during last night's storm. He and his wife, Marie, had both been woken just after midnight when an emergency weather alert sounded on their cell phones. Jake rushed to Alex's room, scooped up his son, and met Marie in the bathroom where they sheltered themselves in the tub until the storm passed. Now, standing on the deck and seeing all the destruction firsthand, Jake realized how lucky they had been.

Taking a sip of coffee, something moved in his periphery and he looked to see his neighbor, Donald Shelor, standing in the middle of his own yard—hands on his hips—assessing the aftermath. Jake turned to flee back inside before being noticed when Don called to him.

"You there... Boy!" Don yelled in his usual gruff and overly stern voice that grated on Jake.

Jake closed his eyes for a moment and took a deep breath before turning back around to face the man.

"Morning, Don," he replied into his cup before taking a sip of coffee.

Watching the man march across their adjacent lawns, Jake was reminded of the first time they met, which had been three years earlier on the day he and his family first moved to Lordsland. They arrived early in the morning and planned to have the oversized U-Haul unloaded by noon. Jake was using a hand truck to maneuver the family's large, side-by-side refrigerator down the ramp of the moving truck when Don appeared out of nowhere. Jake didn't know it at the time, but his neighbor seemed to wear a permanent sneer on his face—at least it was there any time he had the pleasure of speaking to the man, face to face.

"Guess you're moving in, huh?"

Holding the fridge at bay by sheer luck, Jake said, "Yeah. I guess we are."

Don nodded in an exaggerated manner while keeping constant eye contact. "Great, great... Hey, while I've got you here, I wanted to make sure we could sync up our lawn maintenance schedules. You see, if we can keep to a routine, I feel that the neighborhood..."

Jake tuned the man out as he readjusted his grip on the hand truck, nearly tilting the fridge off the ramp in the process.

"...and between you and me, I don't care what they say on TV. I'm not buying some foreign piece of sh—"

"Sorry, uh..."

"Don."

"Don. But now's not a good time," Jake offered as beads of sweat broke out all over his face and were starting to drip into his eyes, causing them to sting.

He saw the man's face harden, and his lip twitch ever-so-slightly. "Fine," Don replied before walking off without another word.

That was their first interaction as neighbors, with many like it since. As Don was about to reach the deck, Jake imagined he'd be adding another tally mark to the encounter board.

"Got a bit of a predicawink here, Ward," Don said in a serious tone.

Jake rolled his eyes—at least inwardly—at what he liked to call "Donisms," which were his neighbor's veiled attempts to launch a passive aggressive attack by combining two words into something nonsensical.

"Oh? What's that, Donald?" Jake replied, knowing the man hated to be called by his full name on informal occasions.

"I'll tell you what. All your damned shit has magically migrated over to my yard!"

Jake took another sip of coffee and looked to where the man was pointing. "Hmm, so it has. Well, I guess there *was* a nasty storm that blew through here last night..."

Don glowered. "Well, I need it cleaned up." His face began to flush with anger.

Jake slurped his coffee extra loud. "I'll, uh, get right on that."

He and his neighbor locked eyes for a moment—Don throwing down the challenge, and Jake accepting without hesitation.

He grinned to himself when Don turned and walked away, mumbling something incoherently. "Prick," Jake retorted as he finished the last dregs of his coffee.

Taking a better look at what Don was talking about, Jake saw that pretty much everything that had been in his backyard was now on his neighbor's property. The swimming pool and the trampoline might prove tricky to move by himself.

Jake massaged the bridge of his nose before walking back into the house to refill his mug. Waiting for the Keurig to heat up, he walked into the living room and turned on the TV to check the morning news.

"...and local meteorologists are still baffled by last night's sudden, and in some places, devastating storm. Emergency responders are still trying to ensure the safety of the residents of Lordsland, while also dealing with normal calls from individuals unaffected by the storm. Mayor Hamm issued a statement this morning for all citizens to only use 911 services for life threatening situations, and furthermore, urged everyone to shelter in place until an all clear is sounded, giving responders more leeway for quicker movement while they travel."

Jake added creamer to his freshly brewed coffee and took a sip, burning his lips in the process. He reached over and clicked the TV off as the news anchor was saying something about upcoming Halloween events around town.

Opening his laptop, he did a quick check of his emails, saw it was empty aside from the usual spam, and opened a blank word document, waiting for inspiration to hit. Jake didn't know how long he stared at the white screen, fingers poised over the keyboard ready to transcribe any creative thought that popped into his head. Yet, his mind remained as empty as the screen in front of him. Closing his eyes and rubbing his temples, the pressure to produce something—anything—was becoming unbearable.

"Fuck it," he uttered, closing the laptop before getting up to get dressed.

Lacing up his sneakers, Jake mentally prepared himself for another round with Don. Stepping back out onto his deck, he took inventory of what he needed to retrieve—which was damn near everything—and went on a scavenger hunt.

Sighing as he stepped off the porch and trudged toward Don Shelor's property, pretending he didn't notice the eagle-eyed man standing in the window, cloaked by the curtains and watching every movement he made, Jake started by collecting Alex's toys that looked as though they'd been knocked out of a battered pinata.

While Jake was busy rescuing his property from Don's yard across town, Anita Jenkins was sitting down for her usual breakfast of Pop-Tarts, cigarettes, coffee, and, of course, the mini NCIS marathon USA Network aired during weekdays. She'd circled around the sun sixty-seven times already, and in all that time, no one caught her attention quite like Mark Harmon did.

Anita was halfway through her second Poptart—and three cigarettes in—when the picture on her TV froze. Something sounded from the kitchen, which caused her to look. She stamped her cigarette butt out in the overfilled ashtray and was about to rise from her chair when the TV unfroze, its volume blaring three times louder than she remembered it being. Startled by the sudden blast of sound, she plopped back down and grabbed the remote, muting it.

Turning in her chair, she perked her ears and listened for the sound again. When she didn't hear anything unusual, Anita chalked it up to being so high-strung since the kid from down the street had called her a "busted old bumper pug." She had no clue what that meant—his intent to insult was clear enough, though—so she had no qualms about cackling the way she did when he hit the curb with his bike and went tumbling over the handlebars.

Anita was about to unmute the TV and turn down the volume when the noise sounded again from the kitchen, this time more distinct and semi-recognizable.

"What the shit was that?" she barked as she lunged out of the recliner.

Facing the kitchen, she scanned the darkness for a moment. Nothing stood out to her as she took an apprehensive step forward. Anita caught herself holding her breath, straining to hear any tell-tale signs of an intruder. Releasing her lungs slowly, she took another step and froze when a meow issued out of the darkness. Her knees weakened and she had to brace herself on the nearby wall to stay upright.

The meow was familiar, distinct—and impossible.

"It... it can't be. F-Floofy? Baby?" Anita questioned, just above a whisper.

Another meow came from the dark and her hand rose, shaking, and covered her mouth. Her mind clouded with memories of Floofy and the pain she'd endured after finding her cat of fifteen years dead one morning, three months earlier. Her constant companion for a decade and a half, Anita spent day in and day out bonding, sharing every waking moment with that cat—a bond she'd never developed with another human—and she knew Floofy's signature meow quite well.

Tears welled in her eyes as she thought about the loneliness since the cat's death. And now, against all rational thinking, she could've sworn her deceased cat was waiting in the kitchen to be fed, just as he always did around this time of day.

Well, it's happened. You've done lost the last few marbles you still had and you think your dead cat has now come back to life and wants to be fed, she thought.

Attempting to reclaim her sanity, Anita called to the cat's name and patted her leg just as she would have when Floofy was alive.

"Psst, psst, psst... here, boy. Here, Floofy. Come to Mama."

She watched the veil of darkness in the doorway of the kitchen, not knowing what she expected—or wanted—by calling out.

Another meow came, this time intermingled with a purr the way Floofy would do when he was happy and content. Caught unprepared, Anita gasped when Floofy—her sweet boy—stepped into the light of the living room. The three months in between their last interaction had not been kind to the cat. Most of Floofy's hair had long since fallen out, and in some spots—head, legs, tail—alabaster-hued bone peeked through where skin was no longer present.

"No! No, you get away from here," Anita cried, her knees buckling again from the sight of the cat.

Floofy's head tilted to one side as if confused, and then stretched out, finishing by digging its claws into the carpet and pulling up strands of it, like it was sharpening them. The cat meowed again—long and deep.

Anita's knees finally gave out and she slid down the wall, never taking her eyes off the cat. Her head snapped from side to side as she wondered how any of this was possible. She had never been much of a horror movie fan, but she'd seen something just like this, years ago, and it sometimes crept into her dreams when she least expected it.

Floofy stepped closer to the distraught woman and began purring. The sound had an unnatural rattle to it, causing Anita to recoil further from the cat's advance. Stepping next to her exposed legs, Floofy brushed his face against them like he did when alive, only this time, instead of tickling her playfully with its whiskers, the cat left a few of them behind—along with decaying bits of flesh.

Floofy meowed, causing Anita to yelp in surprise. Tears streamed down her cheeks, seeing the state of her once faithful companion. The cat meowed a second time and started to paw at her leg like it did every morning in an attempt to rouse her from sleep.

"I-I don't have any food for you. Not since you... died," she croaked.

Floofy looked up at her with his dull, milky eyes and meowed louder.

"I don't have any. P-please, just g-go away."

The rattling purr intensified, and Anita felt five sharp pricks in her leg. The cat slowly drug its paw downward, rending her flesh as it did. She was already against the wall, but Anita tried to pull her legs closer to her chest.

Floofy meowed again, this time—to Anita—it carried an edge.

"Stop it," she cried, her hand slick with blood from her leg.

MEOW!

"Leave!"

Meeooow

"Go! Just go!" she screamed.

Floofy pawed the arm she was using to protect her legs. Claws injected themselves into her paper-thin skin, shredding it as the cat pulled away.

"Please, stop," Anita whimpered as she squeezed her eyes shut. "You died. You're dead."

Meow

Floofy rubbed against her torn flesh, the dead cat's abrasive tongue lapping up blood leaking from the wound. Anita reacted to the jolt of pain, swinging her arm wildly. The cat jumped clear of her arm, still purring, and meowed again.

"Just get the fuck out of here!"

With her adrenaline pumping, she tried to stand, but her legs were still too weak to support her. On hands and knees, Anita started to crawl toward her chair with an end table next to it, and the telephone. She grunted when she felt Floofy's weight press down on her as the cat jumped onto her back. Searing pain made her screech as ten claws burrowed in. Anita began to jerk and spasm as Floofy plucked the flesh along her spine, kneading her tender meat. Every time a claw plunged in, she felt her skin grow taught and then rip as it was pulled out.

Without thinking, she went prone and rolled over, forcing the cat to leap away. Each breath was a struggle as Anita felt warm blood seeping from the wounds, soaking into her shirt.

She gasped when Floofy pounced onto her chest and started the kneading process all over again.

"You little asshole. Stop!"

Mustering enough energy, Anita raised an arm, ready to swipe the demonic visage of her once beloved feline away, when she was halted as the undead cat raked its claws over her face.

Anita bucked in agony as she held her hands over her face, the ocular jelly from her ruined eyes now oozing through her bloodied fingers. Stiffening as she felt a sharp pain shoot through her chest, she released the air in her lungs with a low, gurgling sigh as her heart finally gave out.

A few moments later, a knock came from the front door before it started to creak open.

"Ms. Jenkins, are you decent?" asked the mail carrier. "I've got a pack... sweet Jesus!"

Robert Dale stood frozen in place as he took in the scene before him. A loud meow issued from the dark kitchen, causing the package to slip from his hands as he jumped in fright. Looking back down at the dead woman, Robert saw the package came to rest next to her, already soaking up the pooling blood as it spread over the floor.

Meow!

He ran.

Marie Ward watched as an ambulance went screaming by before entering the elementary school to drop off her son.

"Wonder what that's all about?" she asked Julia, the secretary.

"Hard to tell. How are you doing today, champ?" Julia asked Alex.

Alex didn't answer, just shrugged as he stood next to his mother, his eyes lingering on the entrance where the ambulance just drove by.

"He's still a little shaken from last night. Honey, Julia asked you a question."

"He's fine. How about you join the others in the cafeteria? First period will be starting soon," Julia said as she smiled at him.

Alex nodded solemnly for a moment before walking away. He was almost out of the room when Marie said, "Hey, too big to give your old mom a hug?"

Alex looked around to see if anyone was watching as he walked back to her and gave in to his mom's request. She ruffled his hair and said, "See you at four."

Alex hung his head as he left. Waiting until he was fully out of earshot, Marie turned to Julia and sighed.

"I take it you still haven't had the time to talk to that husband of yours yet?" Julia asked, leaning back in her chair.

Marie closed her eyes and took a deep breath. "I just haven't found the right moment."

Julia laughed. "Could you pass the potato salad, please? Oh, and by the way, I've been fucking the lawn guy behind your back all summer," she blurted in a mocking tone.

"Shh. I can't believe I told you," Marie said, rubbing her palms over her face.

Julia flashed a false look of shock. "Ouch, bitch. Besides, who else are you going to tell all the saucy details to that won't go running to everyone in town and blab about it? Hmm?"

Marie propped herself up on Julia's desk. "I wish it didn't happen."

Julia smirked. "While I can sympathize with you—on both reasonings—it is what it is. But you have to either come clean, or stop letting that guy plow your garden."

"Gross," Marie sighed as she continued to rub her face.

"By the way... have there been any more... *encounters* since the last time?" Julia asked.

Groaning and looking through her fingers, Marie moved her hands to the back of her neck.

"You skank!" Julia chirped. "Out with the details," she said, perking up to listen.

Jake arrived back at the house after liberating all of his property from Don's yard—the pool and trampoline proving to be exceptionally difficult as a one-man job. Most of the items had been covered in mud, so he jumped in the shower to clean up. After toweling off, he checked his emails again before getting cozy—preparing to work on his novel that was approaching a deadline.

As his fingers gently grazed the keys—still waiting for inspiration to strike—a loud hum drew his attention. Setting his laptop to the side, he walked to one of the large windows that looked out over the front lawn and saw the boy from down the street, who was working odd jobs around the neighborhood while home from college. The boy had a weed whacker in his hands and had it going full-tilt, but remained in the same spot, his eyes avoiding the ground as they lingered on the front door of the house.

"What the fu..."

Jake was about to go out and see why he thought the lawn needed trimming the day after a tornado ripped through town, but stopped when he saw his wife's car pull into the driveway. He watched as she crossed the yard and started talking to the kid after he turned off the grass trimmer.

A few times, her head turned toward the house while they talked, finally ending with the guy walking off—his shoulders slumped as he looked back a few times like a lonesome puppy.

Jake returned to the couch and picked up his laptop as Marie walked through the door.

"Hey," he said, pretending to be focused on writing.

"Hey," she replied.

"Was that the kid from down the street out there weed eating?" Jake asked nonchalantly.

"Kid? He's twenty-two. But yeah, crazy, right?" Marie answered as she walked into the kitchen.

"Mmhmm."

"What do you want for dinner tonight?" she asked, opening the fridge, then the freezer.

"Whatever. I don't care."

Jake stared at the blank screen, listening as his wife rummaged around in the kitchen. He'd been on edge for the last few days ever since he'd received a letter in the mail earlier in the week with a fore-closure notice on their home.

He felt like such a failure as a writer, compounded with the guilt of letting the bills pile up until they started to turn into nasty threats of canceled services, and then hiding them before Marie had a chance to see them.

Now, the pressure to produce a masterpiece was bogging him down even more, miring him in doubt and self-pity.

Closing his eyes, Jake envisioned his family out on the street, his wife and son begging for change from passersby as he attempted to scratch out a story in the dirt with an old spork.

"Did you hear me?" Marie asked.

"What?"

"I said I needed some money to pick up a few things from the store," she reiterated.

"Okay." Jake set his computer aside and got up to get his wallet. "How much do you think?"

"Fifty should cover it," she said as she walked over and stood next to him.

Jake saw he only had two twenties and his stomach dropped. "This is what I have on me," he told her as he handed over the bills.

"Okay. Give me your card and I can swing by the ATM while I'm out."

Chewing on his lip, Jake released the breath he'd been holding in.

"I think we should talk about some things."

Marie started to chew her lip as well.

Chapter Two

Paul had arrived at Clint's house, pounding on the door, ripping Clint out of his dream-state before the sun even crested over the hills. Clint sat bitterly at the table, sipping coffee from a steaming mug while thinking about the dream he'd been having. He had been tossing back beers at Slater Lake when the Reed twins that worked down at Donna's Diner popped up from the water, seemingly out of nowhere—each wearing a string bikini that left little to the imagination.

The twins giggled and jiggled, and Clint was speechless as he watched them approach. Each of them placed a hand on his shoulders and proceeded to dance around him. Whenever Clint would try and speak, one of them would place a finger over his lips, while the other would bring a can of beer up and make him drink.

Crushing the empty and tossing it aside before belching, Clint bent toward the cooler to grab another before Cindy Reed's long leg shot out and pushed him back in place. Lou-Anne Reed bent over the cooler—allowing Clint to catch a glimpse of Heaven—and grabbed a frosty can from inside. Cindy slapped her twin's ass—causing her to yelp in surprise, and in turn, causing Clint to whoop with delight. Lou-Anne popped the tab and a cascade of foamy suds erupted all over her face and chest.

"Oops," Lou-Anne giggled with a devilish smile.

Cindy stepped beside her twin. "I swear. What am I gonna do with you? Should I clean her up?" she asked Clint.

Clint nodded with enthusiasm, watching as Cindy's tongue parted her lips, aimed for her beer-soaked twin.

Clint's head swam with lustful desire.

BAM! BAM! BAM!

Pulling his eyes away from the twins, Clint looked around the lake for whatever was making the ruckus. Lou-Anne's moaning drew his attention again and he squirmed when he saw Cindy Reed running her tongue down her twin's stomach.

"HO-LEE-SHI—"

BAM! BAM! BAM!

Clint groaned as he opened his eyes and rolled over, trying to untangle himself from his blankets. The darkness surrounding him was a stark contrast to the evening lake sexcapade from his dream.

BAM! BAM! BAM!

Dragging himself out of bed, Clint grabbed the shotgun he kept next to the nightstand and went to see who was beating down his door.

"Planning to club someone with that thing?" Paul expressed as Clint opened the door, shotgun held ready.

"No. It's loaded," Clint replied.

"Ain't talkin' 'bout the shotty, partner."

Looking down, Clint saw he had an erection standing proud. He sighed as he stood aside, allowing Paul to walk into his house.

"What in God's name are you doin' here this early?"

Paul pulled out a chair at the kitchen table and sat, kicking his feet up and rubbing his knee. "Big storm rolled through last night. Didn't ya notice?"

"Shit no. Tied one on."

"Big storm means power lines down. Power lines down means copper. And copper means money in our pockets," Paul said, matter-of-factly.

Walking over and setting the shotgun on the table, Clint searched the floor until he found the pants he'd shed the previous night.

"Our pockets?" Clint scoffed.

"Well, I mean, you do still owe me for bailing you out the pokey last month," Paul replied, leaning back in the chair.

Clint didn't feel the need to remind his partner in crime that it was, in fact, his fault that he wound up in jail in the first place, since it was Paul's job to stand lookout while Clint raided the dumpster behind Wal-Mart. It was the second biggest shock of Clint's life to come up from the dive, holding a busted vacuum in one hand, and a wad of returned bras in the other, only to find himself staring down the barrel of Sheriff Shipley's .357 magnum—Paul nowhere in sight.

Slapped with a fine and twenty hours of community service, Clint was free again.

Pulling on his boots, Clint grunted as he thought about the last time Paul had taken him out to harvest copper from power lines.

"You sure the lines are down out there?"

"Positive. That storm made a mess of things. And you know the best part of all?"

"What?" Clint asked and shrugged.

"All the police are tied up, dealing with calls coming in from all over the county." Paul grinned as if he were the smartest man alive.

Clint grunted again. "What if they're down, but still juiced?"

Tilting the chair forward, Paul's grin grew wider. "Don't worry about that. I've got that figured out, too." He tilted his head toward the shotgun lying on the table.

Rolling his eyes, Clint stood and stretched. "Let's get after it."

Clapping his hands together, Paul rose and led the way to his truck.

On the road, Clint asked, "Where we headin'?" as he bounced around the cab of Paul's old Ford.

"Foster Farm. Goddamnit, this road is fucked," Paul yipped, hitting a pothole that shook the truck.

Clint braced himself as best he could, but still rang his head off the truck's roof as the two of them rocked and careened down the dirt road.

"Shit," Paul said suddenly, "who the fuck is this?"

Clint looked ahead and saw a beat up old Cavalier sitting on the road. Darting his head around, he didn't see anyone. "Whaddya wanna do? Might be risky," he said.

Paul drummed his fingers on the steering wheel as he thought. "Shiiit, might as well. When opportunity knocks, you answer. Plus we're already out here," he replied, shrugging.

Clint gave his usual grunt as a reply—whether as affirmation or not, it was anyone's guess. Paul eased in behind the Chevy and parked the truck. Exiting the cab, Clint grabbed the shotgun from the seat, while Paul grabbed a duffle bag full of gear from the bed.

"We should head up there. Power lines run right over that old graveyard."

Clint looked to where Paul was pointing. A few of the nearby pylons had been mangled in the storm and it looked to him like the power lines were down, or at least low enough for them to get to.

"Yeah, alright."

Hoisting the duffle bag onto his shoulder, Paul grabbed an old hoe from the back of the truck before leading the way up the hill. As the two of them reached the top, Clint whistled.

"Ho-lee-sheet. This place got tore the fuck up!" he said as he surveyed the demolished cemetery.

"Shit, yeah it did. FUBAR," Paul agreed, tossing his bag to the ground.

"Poor bastards," Clint observed, kicking one of the old, barely legible tombstones. "Cain't even rest in peace."

Paul chuckled as he walked over and looked at the worst part of the destruction. Clint joined him, bending and picking up a shoe that looked out of place in the family cemetery.

"What the..."

"Looks like we're in luck, old boy!" Paul whooped, moving to a nearby tree where a power line lay draped over one of the limbs.

"You think it's hot?" Clint asked.

"Nah, cain't be."

Paul grabbed the line and started to pull, but couldn't get it free from the limb. "Shit, look. It's wrapped around up there. You're gonna have to shimmy up there and cut it down," he said in a huff.

"Wait, what? Climb your fat ass up there and do it," Clint shot back.

Paul looked at him as if offended. "You know I got a bum knee!"

"Since when?"

Scoffing, Paul hobbled over to a half-fallen gravestone and sat, rubbing his leg. "Old football injury, you asshole."

Clint stood and thought for a moment. "That? Wasn't you running laps at tryouts and stepped into a gopher hole or something?"

"It was a groundhog hole. A big one! And my knee ain't been right since. Tweaks every time it rains." Paul winced as he continued to rub his leg, playing it up as much as he could.

Releasing a heavy sigh, Clint relented. "Fine. What am I using to cut it?"

A slight smile flickered across Paul's face as he pointed to the duffle bag. "Got everything you need in there."

Clint walked over and unzipped the bag. A pair of threadbare gardening gloves sat at the top, and a pair of tin snips just underneath them.

"You've gotta be fuckin' kiddin' me," Clint said under his breath and shook his head.

Looking over at Paul, who had now rolled up his pants legs and was comparing his knees, Clint grabbed the gloves and snips before walking to the tree.

With the gloves on—a few fingers wiggling through holes—and snips in his back pocket, Clint began climbing. It was easy enough, and he found himself staring at the power line that was now within arm's reach.

"Hey, you sure this thing is dead?" Clint yelled down to Paul.

Paul looked up from where he sat and nodded. "You saw me yankin' on it. Hold on, lemme test it."

Clint watched as his friend limped over and grabbed the hoe. Continuing on to where the power line lay close to the ground, Paul tested it again by swinging the hoe, striking the line a few times. On the last strike, Clint saw Paul stiffen and start to shake before screaming.

"Oh fuck! Paul? Paul, you okay?" Clint hollered, ready to jump from the tree to save him.

Paul stopped shaking, turned his head slowly, and cracked a not-so-toothy grin before he started howling with laughter.

"You big, dumb, motherfuckin' prick!" Clint exclaimed, glowering.

"Just a goof. Settle down, you pud. It's good, I can see the copper wiring."

Clint wanted nothing more than to give Paul a double dose of his signature birds, but couldn't risk loosening his grip on the tree. Settling for a rabbit punch when he was back on the ground, he retrieved the tin snips from his back pocket and began cutting on the line.

He was nearly through the first layer—while Paul moaned about his knee on the ground below—when he heard a cracking sound from behind. Fearing the limb was buckling under his weight, he turned slowly to see the impossible—a rotted corpse was reaching for him from one of the branches above. Without thinking, he shifted away from the outstretched, skeletal fingers and felt the limb finally give.

Clint tried to grab the power line, but squeezed his eyes shut as it slipped through his fingers. The weightlessness he felt in the brief fall was surreal, but as he slammed onto the ground, the wind was knocked out of him in the form of a yelp.

"You dumb sumbitch. You didn't even cut it all the way through," Paul said as he walked toward Clint.

Rolling onto his back, Clint looked up at the tree—trying to refill his lungs with short gasps—and saw there were actually three corpses scattered in the thicket of branches above.

When the... How the fu... he thought when Paul's head popped into view.

"Git up. Help me yank on this." Paul had grabbed the line and was tugging on it. When Clint tried to speak, only a hiss came out. He pointed at the tree above in an attempt to warn Paul.

"Yeah, I know. You didn't cut the shit all the way."

Clint shook his head and rolled over to his stomach before pushing himself up to his hands and knees.

"No... you... idiot..."

"Heeey," Paul said, sounding incredulous.

"Look u—"

Before Clint could finish, something slammed onto his back, forcing him back to the ground. Dazed by the impact, his senses were lit on fire when something bit into his leg. Screeching from the pain, he looked and saw one of the corpses—very much moving—was now latched onto his calf, gnawing through flesh and muscle.

"Jee-suss Christ!" he yelled.

As he kicked the ruined head of the thing that was eating him, Clint's attention was drawn to his left when he heard the dull thud of something hitting the ground. With a quick glance, he saw another reanimated body stirring to life that had fallen from the tree.

"Paul, fucking help me!" he hollered.

Seeing his friend run out of his view, Clint turned his attention back to the one at his leg. Using his other foot to hold off the one that had taken a huge chunk out of his leg, he felt a quick tug on his left hand and pulled it in close. Blood spurted from the stumps that used to be his pinky and ring fingers, and splashed his face.

The one from his left was now close enough Clint could hear it crunch his finger bones as it chewed, and waves of putrid stench rolled out of the corpse's mouth, assaulting his nose.

Blood continued to pulse out in spurts, but Clint had no choice but to use his maimed hand to halt the hungry ghoul's progress. Reaching out, he flat-palmed the forehead of the once living person, feeling his hand sink inward until skull fragments shifted enough for a firmer hold.

"I'm comin'," Paul shouted.

Doing his best to maintain the balance of fending off the undead assailants, Clint chanced a look and saw Paul racing toward them with the hoe poised over his head, ready to strike.

"Ahhhh!" Paul yelled like a warrior charging into battle.

Clint watched as the hoe arched in the air above, flinching and squeezing his eyes closed, bracing for whatever happened next. A loud crack sounded to his right and he heard Paul curse. Clint looked and saw Paul standing, staring at the broken end of the hoe shaft. In the tree above, another corpse shambled down from the higher limbs, its face contorted with menace, catching Clint's attention just before it dropped.

"Oh sheeeeet!" he yelled, bracing himself.

The impact came and grave dirt and human dust filled his airways—with a sharp pain erupting in his midsection—causing him to cough and struggle for air. A bone from the corpse that fell from the tree had jutted out from its rotten stomach and pierced Clint in his belly. The undead at Clint's leg was able to break through his resistance, while the one to his left now had his arm pinned. Reaching out for help from Paul, the two locked eyes for a moment before Paul threw the broken handle to the ground and raced away in the other direction—hurdling a few tombstones as he went.

"Sonofabi—" Clint started to say before moaning at the pain in his abdomen.

With the one at his leg gnawing on him like a dog with a bone, and the other trying to finish what it had started with his fingers, Clint watched as the third reanimated corpse of one of the long-dead Fosters crawled around on his chest, twisting the bone in Clint's guts, churning his innards. Blackened shards peeked out of its maw, and the milky remnants of the thing's eyes caused him to scream one last time for help.

Broken teeth sank into his neck and Clint felt the warm rush of blood cascading down his skin.

The last thought to flash through Clint's mind as the world darkened around him was how fast Paul fled—like the wind, both knees unhindered.

Jake hammered his fist on the dashboard as he sped down the road. His mind was racing and nothing made sense anymore. The bombshell Marie dropped on him that she'd been fucking the lawn guy had blindsided him so much so that, if he hadn't left the house, he didn't know what he would've done.

Drive.

That was the only thing he could think to do. The only thing that made sense. And with no destination in mind, he was on autopilot.

"I have to tell you something..."

"You have to understand, I have needs, too..."

"Why are you staring at me like that? Say something!"

Over and over, her words replayed in his head. Over and over, his heart clinched in his chest when he thought of the look of anger she wore, a mask covering the Marie he knew and loved.

With a deep sigh, Jake turned his attention to the radio in an attempt to distract himself. His wife's country music station assaulted his ears and caused him to grimace. Turning the dial, Jake found a classic rock station.

Looking back to the road, a blur came from his left, forcing him to stomp on the brakes. A man darted across the road as Jake looked on in disbelief.

"You fucking asshole," he yelled while laying on the horn and holding the gas pedal to the floor. Tires barked as he pulled away.

Up ahead, he saw a sign for the local watering hole, *McGoo's,* and slowed before easing into the parking lot.

"A drink sounds really fucking good right about now," he said to himself, killing the engine.

Stepping into the dank, hazy bar, Jake looked around for a moment before sitting down on one of the stools at the counter.

"What'll it be?" the bartender asked, her voice raspy despite her cuteness.

Swallowing hard, he looked away for a moment, embarrassed by his lack of knowledge about alcohol and said, "Whatever's on tap. And a shot of whiskey."

The bartender stood—unblinking—before reaching for a glass. Returning with his beer and shot, she stood for a moment—eyeing him—before moving down the bar to tend to one of the other patrons.

Without hesitating, Jake picked up the whiskey and tossed it back. It had been years since he'd drunk hard liquor in any serious capacity—long before Marie and Alex became his life's purpose—but the whiskey had bite, and he choked as it burned its way down his throat.

A man chuckled and slapped Jake on the back as he moved onto the stool to Jake's right. "Easy does it, boy. Don't be in no hurry. Still early in the day, so pace yourself."

Jake scoffed. "Easy for you to say, old timer."

The old man raised his eyebrows and nodded. "Not wrong. Not right, but not wrong, either. Lady problems, I'm guessing."

Jake shot the man a side-glance and rolled his eyes. He really wasn't in the mood to talk about it, or listen to any pearls of wisdom spewed out by an alcoholic, Gandalf-looking, midday boozehound. Raising his beer in the air, Jake downed half the glass in two gulps. Belching loudly, he stared ahead, letting the alcohol go to work at numbing his mind.

"Alright, alright. I get it. You don't need a shoulder to cry on. How about another round on me?" the old man offered.

Jake shrugged before saying, "Sure."

He noticed the stranger was grinning before he whistled and waved to the bartender. "Another round for me, and whatever my new friend here wants."

Jake called for the same order before turning slightly to better face the old man. "Okay, what's your story? You don't look as though you have a pot to piss in, but here you are, offering to buy drinks for someone you don't even know."

The stranger chuckled softly. "Name's Mavid. I could tell by the look on your face—whether you want to admit it or not—that things in your life are going south. And fast. Everyone faces tribulations, best not to go it alone. A friend is what you need, and a friend I'm here to be."

Instantly softening the hard exterior he was projecting, Jake appreciated the man's kindness. Often, he felt there was something missing in his life that he couldn't quite put his finger on. He had work, and when he wasn't pounding away on the keyboard, there was Marie and Alex to fill his time. *But where is my time?* he thought.

And then his thoughts turned to Marie and her confession. The images of his wife and that greasy-haired, punkass yard boy doing god knows what in their bed while he was out trying to provide as best he could for his family made his blood boil.

"Fuck!" Jake said, not realizing it was audible.

"Yep, definitely woman problems," Mavid confirmed.

Jake rubbed his hands over his face before leaning forward and resting his head against the bar.

"There, there," Mavid said. "It happens to the best of us. Best thing to do is raise a glass and let the memories be memories."

This guy really is like Gandalf, Jake thought.

Sitting up, Jake picked up the new shot of whiskey and held it out for a toast. "To memories. May they rot in hell."

"To memories," Mavid replied, clinking his glass with Jake's.

Chapter Three

Sheriff Shipley rolled his eyes as he held the phone receiver to his shoulder, still able to hear Anita Donavan jawing on about what fifty other residents of Lordsland had already called in for this morning. Clearing his throat, he brought the phone back up to his ear.

"Mrs. Donavan, I assure you we're doing our best to respond to everyone in as timely a fashion as possible. We are very aware of the tornado that came through town last night and have to take on each case based on the severity of the situation."

"Severity of the situ..." Anita started. "I told you about my situation! I'm a taxpayer, you know?"

Shipley grumbled. "Yes, Mrs. Donavan, but your missing porch swing isn't something we have the manpower to investigate currently. We're spread thin as it is already."

The woman on the other end of the call made a disgusted sound in his ear. "Maybe you should increase your *manpower* if you're having trouble doing your job!'

Shipley bit his tongue before replying. "You are absolutely right, Mrs. Donavan. And as you said, being the nice tax paying citizen that you are, I would hope you add a little extra the next time you go to pay them. Thank you, Mrs. Donavan. Call back with any *urgent* matters."

As he hung the receiver back on its cradle, Sheriff Shipley could hear the woman giving her added two cents about paying more taxes.

Leaning back in his chair, he could see his two deputies, as well as his secretary, engaged in their own verbal battles to placate the unrest brought on by the freak of nature storm. Stretching, he stood and grabbed his hat from the nearby coat rack. Holstering his sidearm, Shipley left his office.

"Gonna head out and assess the damage firsthand, Barb. You can get me on the radio if you need anything."

His matronly secretary nodded as she continued on with her phone call. Tipping his hat to the deputies, he headed for the door.

Stepping into the sunlight, he surveyed downtown Lordsland, noting the lack of traffic. Any other day, Main Street would be bustling, but since the storm rolled through, and the request from Mayor Hamm to keep the roads clear, folks seemed to be taking the advice and staying home.

His police cruiser was parked along the side of the station. Shaking his keys out of his pocket, Shipley was about to unlock the door when he heard feet pounding down the pavement, heading his way. Instinct made his hand jump for the gun on his hip.

Edging back around the front of the station, he saw one of the local troublemakers racing toward him.

"What's up, Paul?" the sheriff called, waving with his freehand in the air.

Paul drew short of where Shipley stood, his chest heaving to take in oxygen. "I-uh... There's-uh... Clint-uh..."

The hair on the back of Shipley's neck stood on end as he approached the distraught man. "Slow down. Breathe. Start from the beginning."

Paul doubled over for a moment as he attempted to catch his breath, finally straightening. Shaking his head, he said, "Fuck it..." as he collapsed to the ground.

"Jesus fucking Christ," Shipley said before calling back toward the station for help.

Marie couldn't blame her husband for his reaction after hearing the news she'd been cheating on him with their lawn care guy. What she was more miffed about was the blank expression he wore after his initial outburst. After the screaming "Whys?" and "How could this happen?", he'd swept everything sitting on the dining table onto the floor and then went still—as if a switch had been flipped inside him. Marie watched as Jake calmly walked into the living room, grabbed his keys, and left without speaking another word.

Now, sitting on the floor amongst the broken shards from a flower vase and cracked family photos, Marie was nursing her third Jack Daniels since his departure. She had a healthy buzz going, numbing away any thoughts of the fallout that was sure to come once Jake returned home. Her thoughts shifted to Alex and what he would think of her. She felt she'd betrayed him just as much as her marriage.

Wallowing in her self-inflicted sorrow, Marie tossed back the remainder of the Tennessee whiskey that was sloshing around in her glass. She contemplated refilling it again, but knew she couldn't get completely smashed since Alex would be home in a couple of hours.

Lulling her head around, enjoying the added sensation of the already spinning room, she started to hum a song.

A crash on the front porch drew her attention.

"Hwut the fug wassat?" Marie slurred, staring at the front door.

Stumbling to her feet, she worked hard to maintain her balance as she made her way to the door to investigate. Using the peephole, Marie recognized Ethan's sandy blonde hair instantly. Fumbling with the lock, then the doorknob, she opened the door and said, "You can't beee hrr r'now. Jake knows bout us, annn if he findzzz you hrr, he'll kill—"

Marie abruptly stopped talking when Ethan slowly turned around and she saw half of his face was missing. A trembling hand rose to her mouth and stifled a scream before it could escape. Off kilter, she backed away so suddenly, she nearly toppled over a table that stood next to the entranceway.

Ethan lunged at her, narrowly missing as Marie retreated farther into the house. The scream finally erupted from her mouth as she stumbled through the living room, heading for the backdoor.

The shock of the Ethan-thing was sobering her up quickly, but she still staggered and bumped into things—knocking as many obstacles into her wake in hopes of slowing him down—including the kitchen chairs.

Semi-running into the door, Marie was able to open it and slip out right as Ethan's growls came up behind her. The sun blinded her temporarily—using her hand to block it out—and she stood on the deck trying to figure out what to do next.

A crash from behind made her turn and look to find Ethan charging through the storm door, pieces of broken glass now lodged in his chest and face.

Marie yelled for him to stop, but knew he wasn't there, wasn't the same person who'd reignited the passion in her loins. Slowly backing away from him, her situational awareness failed her alcohol addled brain when she took one step too many. Her foot found empty air and sent her four steps worth to the ground, sprawling her flat on her back.

Her whiskey numbed body helped with the brunt of the impact. A shadow loomed over her and she squinted and looked up to see Ethan, just as he tumbled forward. Marie instinctively raised her hands in defense. Pieces of broken glass sticking out of the young man's chest sliced into her hands, exiting out the back as his added weight pinned her to the ground.

Tears of fear and pain flooded her eyes. Ethan's ruined face was inches from hers, his teeth clacking together as he bit the empty air between them. A growl rumbled deep from within his chest. Marie closed her eyes and turned her face away from him, accepting defeat and whatever would come next.

Just before blacking out, she heard a loud thud and prayed Alex wouldn't come home to find what was left of her after Ethan had his way with her, one last time.

Sheriff Shipley and his two deputies were able to haul Paul into the station and set him up on one of the cots in a holding cell.

"Barb, you find one of those smelling things?" Shipley asked.

She was busy pilfering through the station's lackluster, outdated first-aid kit and came back empty-handed. "Nothing in there that's going to help bring him around," Barb replied.

"You said he was running? Like, hard running? Paul?" Brent asked—Shipley's senior deputy.

The sheriff nodded. "Yeah, like a bat out of hell."

"Which way did you see him come from?" Deputy Jon asked—Lordsland's newest public servant.

The sheriff had to think for a moment before he said, "West, coming out of Narrow Gap."

"Do you want us to take a ride out that way?" Brent asked. "See if we see anything unusual?"

"Yeah. Do that," Shipley said after considering it for a moment. "And make a round of the whole town while you're at it. Take Bertha with you."

"Roger that, boss," Jon affirmed. "We'll radio in if we find anything."

Brent disappeared into Shipley's office for a moment, returning with a shotgun in his hands. Checking Bertha's breach to see if it was loaded, he nodded to Jon, signaling they were ready to roll.

After the two deputies left the station, Sheriff Shipley attempted to rouse Paul awake. When he failed to do so, he then checked the man to ensure he still had a pulse. With confirmation, he shrugged and left the holding cell.

"Hey, Barb. Can you give Doc Butler a call and see if he can swing by? I don't think Paul is in any immediate danger, but I'd like to have him looked over. And hopefully he'll be awake by then."

Sitting down at her desk, Barb smiled and said, "Sure thing, Sheriff."

Shipley winked playfully and said, "Thanks."

Shuffling back into his office, he took inventory of the small arsenal the station kept. Pickings were slim at the best of times, but with Bertha out in the field, the selection looked down right pitiful. Stroking his chin, Shipley settled on the .38 special and picked it and some extra rounds up before closing the locker.

"Here," he said, holding out the revolver to Barb. "I'm going to head out as well and see what's going on around town. Remember everything I taught you?"

Barb's eyes shifted from Shipley's face to the gun and she grinned. Taking the .38, she popped the cylinder open and spun it, checking to make sure it was loaded. With a quick flick of her wrist, the cylinder slapped back into the frame.

It was Shipley's turn to grin. "You never cease to amaze me, Barb. Radio if you need something, or when Doc Butler shows up."

"Will do," Barb replied.

Just before leaving the police station, Shipley turned and saw his secretary practicing her aim with the gun.

She's a badass, he thought.

"...'s just it, you can't trust fuckin' nobody. Soonasyado, boom! You look like the biggest dumbshit alive," Jake said, sloshing around his drink as he talked more with his arms than his mouth.

Mavid nodded in agreement.

A few more people had filtered into the dive bar since Jake's arrival, but he was too deep into his glass to notice. Now, sufficiently lubed with liquid courage, Jake's caution was completely thrown to the wind as he delved into his newly acquired marital problems.

"I mean, it's not like I haven't wanted to fuck other people, you know? But did I? Absolutely not!"

"Happens to the best of us," Mavid said. "It is what it is."

The sage advice his new friend offered since they began their quest to drink themselves into oblivion made perfect sense to Jake. Struggling to dismantle the barstool and gain his footing, Jake held his arms out—both for balance, and to signal he needed to make an announcement. Everyone that had been listening in on his oversharing tales of woe perked up and waited.

"I... gotta piss."

A few cheers, as well as jeers, followed him as he made his way to the restroom. The closet-sized space reeked of urine, and the overhead lights flickered so badly, it threw Jake's already off-kilter equilibrium into a tailspin. Using his hand to brace himself against the wall, he unzipped his fly and felt the instant relief of his draining bladder.

Watching as his piss swirled down the drain didn't help with Jake's dizziness. Closing his eyes was not an option due to the spins, so he looked at a small window above the dank, decrepit toilet. The window was partially opened and he could see the branches of a tree swaying in the wind.

A smell, not originating in the bar's restroom wafted in, causing Jake to gag and wrinkle his nose. After zipping his fly and washing his hands—drying them on his pants since there were no towels available—he made his way back to his barstool.

"Hey, partner," Jake said to the bartender. "You got something dead and rotting out back. Can smell it comin' in the window."

"Goddamn raccoons again, probably. They get in the dumpster for scraps and get stuck. It's like they have a death pact or something," the bartender said, shaking her head and blowing out a sigh of frustration.

"I had a pet raccoon once. Named it Robb," Mavid said, a forlorn look written on his face. "I used to feed it every morning. Then, one day, it didn't show up. Never saw it again…"

Jake, bowing his head, wiped a solemn tear from his cheek. "That's… that's beautiful, man. I'm so sorry for your loss," he said, patting Mavid's shoulder. "Another for my friend."

He and Mavid toasted to Robb.

As they drank, the bartender told them she'd be back after dealing with the dumpster, grabbing a trash bag before disappearing into the back.

Jake squinted at the clock behind the bar and was shocked to see it was nearly noon. He would need to pick up Alex at two, and in his current state, he doubted he could sufficiently prepare a bowl of cereal without fucking it up.

"That's it for me, I'm afraid," Jake said, placing his half-empty glass on the bar top. "I gotta be somewhere shortly."

"Shiiiit, we was just startin' to drink," Mavid replied.

"I know, I know… Whatcha gonna do, though?"

Crestfallen by the frown on his new friend's face, Jake mirrored the sentiment on his own. Looking up to ask the bartender if she could make him some coffee, he saw she hadn't returned yet.

"Must've been a big fuckin' raccoon," he remarked.

"Yeah. I've seen 'em get as big as a goa—" Mavid started to say, but was cut off when the entrance to the bar swung open with a crash and the bartender came rushing in, slamming the door closed behind her.

"Holy fucking shit!" she said to everyone that was staring at her.

Alex Ward was mid-swing on the monkey bars when Spike Kneeland started to taunt him.

"You'll never make it," Spike yelled.

Alex was four rungs from the end and was determined to make it this time. Keeping with the momentum he had going, he reached and grabbed the next rung. *Three more*, he told himself, his arms starting to ache.

Kicking his feet, Alex gained another rung and was now two away from the end.

"Uh oh, looks like you're getting tired," Spike chided. "Don't slip!"

Alex could feel his palms becoming greasy as he gripped the metal bars. Beads of sweat were starting to pop out on his forehead and streak down his face. Swinging, he grabbed the next rung.

One more. Just one more...

With every ounce of will power his nine-year-old mind could muster, he went for the final rung. His fingers started to slip before he could get a firm grasp. Alex was about to slip away, the rung at his fingertips, when he dug deep and found the strength to wrap his hand around the bar, completing the crossing.

"Yay, great job!"

Cheers came from behind Alex. When he looked, he saw Rachel Meyerson standing there, who'd apparently been watching the whole time.

"I knew he could do it," Spike said, matter-of-factly.

Alex rolled his eyes at Spike before switching his gaze to Rachel, a blush rising on his already reddened cheeks.

He was about to tell her thank you and ask the two of them if they wanted to play tag or something, when screams rang out from the other side of the playground. Alex looked and saw kids running toward them. One of the grown-ups shouted for everyone to get inside.

"What do you think is going on?" Rachel asked.

"I don't know," Alex replied, "but we better go."

Just before they were about to leave the monkey bars, Spike told them to look and pointed at the far treeline.

The three of them stood—planted to the spot—as they watched what looked to be a bunch of people emerging from the woods. One of the grown-ups shouted louder and more forcefully for everyone to get inside.

Alex tugged at Rachel and Spike's sleeves and said he would race them back to the school. Both Spike and Rachel tied—touching the outside wall at the same time—with Alex coming in at a close third. After they were back in their classroom, the murmuring amongst the other kids was overwhelming.

Everyone was cliqued up in their usual grouping of friends, most standing by the windows. Alex fought his way in for his own spot at the window to see what was going on and saw there were now twice as many people outside, all of them wandering around the playground.

None of the strangers looked normal, and he couldn't say what made him think of it, but to him, they looked like something out of a movie or a video game he'd seen on the internet.

To him, they looked like zombies.

Deputies Jon and Brent had driven west after leaving the police station. The town of Lordsland had taken a beating from the storm the previous night, but they hadn't encountered anything that could be considered out of the ordinary.

"Trees, trees, and trees... Nothing but fucking downed trees, from what I see," Brent said, riding shotgun in the cruiser.

"Yeah. Oh, there was that kiddy pool that got impaled on the Streds' mailbox," Jon added.

"Mmhmm."

Pulling up to a stop sign at an intersection, Jon looked left, then right. "Which way do you want to go?"

Brent looked both ways. "I don't care. One is as good as the other."

Jon hesitated for a moment before signaling left.

"Not much this way. That old farm, and the substation," Brent remarked.

His last words hung in the air between them, and they looked at one another for a moment. Knowing what they did about Paul, and the storm that swept through the area, it was a sure bet this was exactly where he'd come from.

"Man, this place got hit hard," Brent acknowledged, craning his head around to look at the destruction.

"Yeah, must be where the tornado touched down," Jon replied, easing the cruiser around a large limb that was laying in the road.

"We'll need to get a clean-up crew out here as soon as possible."

"Want me to call it into Barb?" Brent asked, picking up the radio mic.

"Nah, we'll do it when we get back to the station," Jon said as he shook his head.

Slowing the cruiser to a crawl as they approached the power substation, Jon and Brent looked around the site for any signs of tampering or trespassing, but found it hard to pinpoint anything due to all the fallen limbs and wind-tossed vegetation—keeping anything suspicious from their view.

"Kinda odd," Jon said. "Do you know if there were any reports of power outages anywhere?"

"A few, but nothing major, especially for the kind of storm we had last night. That shit was wild," Brent replied, shifting in the seat to trace the power lines stringing out of the substation.

"Hmm. Well, might as well roll out to the Foster Farm, check things out, then we can head back. If we don't find anything, we don't find anything."

"Right."

Moving on from the substation, the old Foster Farm wasn't far, accessible only by a dirt road that hadn't been very well maintained over the years. They bounced along, Jon doing his best to avoid any fallen debris, ruts, or potholes.

"Well, look what we have here," he said as he pulled up behind Paul's junker.

"Called it!" Brent exclaimed.

The two deputies exited the police cruiser and surveyed the area.

"Wonder whose Chevy that is?" Brent asked, pointing at the Cavalier.

Jon approached the vehicle, rubbing the stubble on his chin. "I think it's that one kid's, the one that works at Applebee's over in Willow Hill."

"Ain't he dating Doc Butler's daughter? Alice, or whatever?"

"Anna. Yeah, that's the one. Wonder why it's parked way out here? And with Paul's jalopy?"

Brent shrugged before bending to look inside. "Bunch of beer cans in the back. Maybe they came out here to party and got caught off-guard by the storm? Only thing close by is that old farmhouse down the road. And a family cemetery up on the hill there."

"Anyone live in the house?" Jon asked.

Brent shook his head. "Nah, I don't think so. Not for years, anyway."

Jon nodded. "Alright, which one do you want to check out? House or cemetery?"

Smirking, Brent said, "Shit, you hike your ass up that hill. I'll check out the house."

Rolling his eyes, Jon started up the newly trodden path. As he did, Brent walked down the dirt road, kicking a stray rock or two along the way.

The dilapidated shack was in such disrepair, Brent doubted the porch would hold his weight without collapsing. Opting to find a different vantage point, he walked around the side of the house and found a grimy window. Cleaning it as best he could, Brent confirmed the place was definitely abandoned by the thick layer of undisturbed dust that covered everything. Satisfied no one was, or had been, at the house, he made his way back to where the police cruiser sat.

Jon still wasn't back yet, so he opened the passenger side door and plopped down onto the seat. Enough time passed that it became noticeable, and there was still no sign of Jon. Sighing, Brent gazed up the hill, making a mental note to kick his fellow deputy's ass for making him go up there.

The higher he hiked, the hotter Brent became, and the bugs were becoming unbearable as he swatted them away from his face.

Nearing the top, a scent assaulted his nose, like an animal had died nearby and had been baking in the hot sun for weeks.

"Hey, Jon! Where the fuck are you?" Brent called.

Surveying the area, Brent was shocked at the destruction caused by the storm way up here. He knew the Foster family cemetery was close by and hoped it wasn't wrecked.

"Jon! Hey, come on!"

Listening for a reply, something shuffled in the brush to his right. His mind yelled danger and his hand snapped to the sidearm he was wearing as he waited to see what it was.

"Jon, if that's you, stop fucking around," Brent said.

The underbrush to the left of where he stood started to shake and he popped the gun free from its holster and took aim. Taking a small step forward, he felt his senses working overtime as adrenaline pumped through his veins.

Again, Brent caught a whiff of decay—stronger than before—and realized a light breeze was blowing on the back of his head. Before he could fully turn around, the thing from the bush was on him—its gaping maw of blackened teeth chomping down on the hand gripping his gun.

Pain shot up his arm, forcing his hand open. Brent quickly took a step back as the gun fell to the ground, leaving a chunk of his hand in the thing's mouth.

"Goddamnit!" he shouted as he pulled his maimed hand to his chest.

Whatever it was that stood in front of him, triggered all the memories he had of staying up late at night as a kid to catch old horror movie marathons.

Brent moved farther away from the putrid corpse standing in front of him and stumbled , but was able to correct his footing before he fell. Looking down, he saw the lifeless body of Jon—his throat was missing and one of his eyeballs had been squished and was leaking ocular jelly onto the bloody grass surrounding his body.

Something broke through the brush behind him and Brent quickly looked and saw three corpses closing in on his position. Without hesitation, he charged at the one that had bit his hand, sending the thing to the ground.

Abandoning hope of retrieving his service pistol, Brent descended to the hill in record time, heading for the cruiser. Smashing into the side of the car—knocking the breath out of his lungs in the process—he chanced a look back and saw no less than seven reanimated corpses in pursuit.

He was in full flight mode until a single word snapped to the forefront of his mind—Bertha.

Brent skidded across the hood and clamored to open the passenger door. His pursuers were closer than he would've liked as the stench of their decay assaulted his nose. Diving in, Brent grabbed the shotgun from the floorboard. As he did, something smashed into the driver's side window, shattering it and sending a shower of broken glass toward him.

Bertha became entangled in his haste and he jerked to free it, catching the trigger by accident, sending a wad of buckshot into the cruiser's radio.

"Fuck!" Brent yelled as he spilled out of the car onto the ground.

Gaining his feet, he saw a group of rotting humans on the other side of the cruiser. Racking a new shell into the breach of the shotgun, Brent took aim—remembering every zombie movie he'd ever seen—at their heads and fired. Two dropped from sight instantly as their skulls blew away into powder.

Pumping in another shell, he started to strafe around the police vehicle to take better aim. Three withered husks were driving at him, too spread out for a conservative shot to save ammo.

Thinking quickly, Brent started to walk backwards in hopes of corralling them where he wanted them to be.

"Gotcha," he said as he pulled the trigger.

Where three heads had once been, now stood pulverized stumps. A cloud of dusted remains hung in the air as the bodies fell to the ground.

Two shambling corpses still remained in front of him. Keeping pace with them, he continued to move away as they progressed. Brent hadn't realized he'd been moving toward the old farmhouse until he was past the Cavalier. Sweat beaded his brow, and his palm started to moisten, making his grip on Bertha slippery.

Three more dead had stumbled off the hillside and joined the others in their pursuit of the deputy. Glancing quickly at the house while maintaining his distance, Brent considered his next move.

If the gun was fully loaded, he thought, *then I should have two shells left.*

He knew it'd be a miracle to take out all five of them with two shots, but what lingered in the back of his mind—a salute to his police training—was not if he could take them all out, but incapacitate as many as he could, giving him better odds.

Turning and jogging ahead to the rickety porch, Brent turned, took aim, and sent buckshot through as many fetid legs as possible. Three of the corpses toppled to the ground, tripping the two that lagged behind.

Breathing the briefest sigh of relief, he chanced the porch behind him—the boards groaning under his added weight—and planted his boot into the front door of the old farm house. Hinges squealed as it swung open, motes of dust jumping into the rays of sunlight cascading in through the filthy windows.

Brent wasted no time entering and slamming the door shut behind him.

He saw the door frame was busted from his kick and searched for something to barricade the door. An old, upright radio cabinet caught his eye. Setting Bertha against the wall, Brent slid the heavy cabinet against the door, hoping it would hold for the time being.

Outside, he heard the corpses clawing their way onto the porch, scratching at the walls and door.

Grabbing Bertha, he retreated farther into the old house. The place was filthy and Brent couldn't recall when the Foster family had last lived here. Evidence of local teens using the place as a party spot littered the floor: beer cans, used condoms, and the occasional whiskey bottle.

He made his way into the kitchen where an old icebox stood open. On the other side of the room was the backdoor that led into the woods. Peeking through the window, goosebumps rippled across his skin when he saw more undead filing out of the trees.

Squeezing Bertha tighter, something above chittered, causing Brent to jump. Looking, he saw there was a larger hole in the ceiling, just above an ancient wood stove. Easing closer to the hole, he looked and could only see darkness.

Another chittering sound raced across the ceiling. Brent quickly shouldered the shotgun, prepared for whatever it was.

Swallowing hard, he stared into the hole and saw no less than two dozen glowing eyes looking down at him.

"Oh shit!" he yelled, firing off his final shell.

The eyes disappeared, but slowly came back into view, one set at a time. Backing away, something slammed into the door that led outside. Doing a quick about-face, Brent pumped the shotgun, aiming at the crusty corpse staring at him through the window, and pulled the trigger. A hollow click filled the room. Pump. *Click*. Pump. *Click*.

"Fuck," Brent said, his heart racing.

Backing away from the door, the hole above him slipped his mind until he heard a screeching sound coming from it. Looking up, all Brent saw was a ball of matted fur coming at him. Before he could react, the thing latched onto his face, clawing away flesh as tiny teeth bit away pieces of his forehead. Flailing, Brent ripped the creature away and flung it across the room. Sheets of blood started to pour down his face and into his eyes. Before his vision was completely obscured, he saw the striped pattern of the gray fur and knew it was a raccoon that had attacked him.

More screeches sounded, and Brent furiously wiped at the blood with his hand. He felt something bite into his calf, and then his ankle, as another dropped onto his shoulder, taking part of his ear as he tossed it away.

Taking a few wild swings with Bertha, his blood-slicked hand did little to help clear his vision when he attempted to clean his eyes. Another raccoon landed on his back from above, tearing at the back of his neck. Slinging the shotgun away, Brent used both hands to grab at it, coming away with handfuls of bristly, rotten fur.

He lunged backwards, hoping to find a wall, and hit his mark; the sound of brittle bones snapping came from behind him. Using his palms, he wiped at his eyes, freeing them of blood for a moment. From the kitchen floor, half a dozen raccoons—each in a different stage of decomposition—looked up at him with ravenous eyes.

"Fuck this!" Brent screamed before fleeing, the sound of claws digging into wood in his wake.

Before he was able to remove the radio cabinet that barricaded the front door, three of the undead critters were on him. Claws swiped and teeth gnashed, and Brent screamed as he went down in a heap. More paws pattered up his body, tearing into his uniform and the flesh underneath with skeletal, needle-sharp claws.

The world around Brent was quickly fading away through a sheen of crimson. With his last conscious thought, he regretted ever thinking these little fuckers were cute.

Chapter Four

The classroom was a whirlwind of chaos as Alex Ward sat quietly at his desk. The other kids were running around, screaming about all the people that wandered out of the woods—including Spike and Rachel. Their teacher, Mrs. Nelson, normally kept the fifteen students under her care in check, but ever since the appearance of the zombies, her face had gone blank, and she sat at her desk, rocking slowly as her lips moved silently, her eyes closed.

"Woah, that one's missing its eyes!" someone yelled.

The other kids all asked where and crowded around the window closest to the kid that had announced it.

"Eww!" a few of them exclaimed.

Alex looked and saw Rachel glancing at him. He wished they wouldn't tap on the glass as if trying to draw the attention of fish in an aquarium. He wished he wasn't here at all, but back home with his mom and dad.

"Children. CHILDREN!" Mrs. Nelson called from the front of the classroom, now standing. "Please, everyone, take your seats."

Alex looked back and saw none of the other kids had moved.

"Now!" Mrs. Nelson barked, more forcefully than Alex had ever heard her be.

Some of the kids complained, echoed by a few others, but ultimately everyone complied with the demand.

Spike slid into his seat in front of Alex—Rachel in the one behind him—and looked back, mouthing, "What's going on?" Alex shrugged and nodded toward Mrs. Nelson.

Steepling her hands in front of her chin, Mrs. Nelson's eyes wandered around the classroom, hopping from face to face, ensuring she held everyone's undivided attention.

"We are in the end times, children." She spoke slowly and deliberately. "I have waited my entire life for this moment to arrive. I have seen this very thing play out in my dreams." Her eyes lingered at the windows for a moment before continuing to pace around the classroom. "My worry is that none of you are properly prepared to receive salvation. That your parents have led you astray, wandering aimlessly off of His golden path."

Rachel and Alex exchanged a look of confusion, mixed with unease, as Mrs. Nelson continued.

"Your innocence must remain intact if you're to witness paradise in all its glory, children. I will be your shepherd. The one that will ensure your souls are rescued from the clutches of eternal damnation."

All eyes remained on Mrs. Nelson as she walked across the classroom and locked the only door that provided an exit. A click rang out and Alex saw a few of the others stir, squirming in their seats.

Returning to her desk, Mrs. Nelson faced the class, a grim, dower look on her face. She closed her eyes and started shaking her head.

"Join me in prayer, children. If you do not know how, follow my example."

Mrs. Nelson started saying the prayer loud enough for everyone to hear her. Spike watched for a moment—making sure he wouldn't be noticed—and turned to face Alex and Rachel.

"I think she's gone crazy," he whispered, just loud enough for them to hear.

Alex nodded and Rachel said, "I don't like this. Why did she lock the door?"

"I don't know, but I want to go home. Those things out there, they're like zombies or something," Alex replied.

"Yeah, that's it. They are zombies, like in Minecraft. Shit..." Spike said, agreeing with Alex.

The volume of Mrs. Nelson's voice rose and the three of them hushed, turning to look at her. Their teacher's brow was so furrowed, looking as though she had one singular eyebrow. When her tone normalized, Spike turned around again.

"We need to get outta here."

Alex rubbed his hands on his pants. "Yeah, but how? And when we do, what about all those dead people outside?"

Puzzled defeat swept over Spike's face as he thought about what Alex said. The two of them were drawn back—having been lost in thought—when Rachel spoke. "I think I know a way we can get past them."

Alex and Spike looked at each other, then at Rachel in unison, their eyebrows raised in intrigue. Grinning, Rachel opened her notebook and started writing, her eyes focused with concentration.

Marie sat in the passenger seat of Don Shelor's car, watching the houses slip by as they drove down the road. Her hands throbbed in dull pain, and she couldn't bear to close her eyes due to the fact that every time she did, Ethan's bloody, mangled face was there, trying to eat her.

She side-eyed Don for a moment, watching as his head darted around like a hawk, taking in every little bit of their surroundings while he drove her to the doctor's office. Marie had never liked the man, him being who he was made it easy, but she begrudgingly looked at him with a newfound appreciation after he'd come to her rescue earlier. Had it not been for him standing vigil at his window and seeing her fleeing from her summer fling, springing into action with an umbrella he kept handy near the back door, she would've died right then and there in her backyard.

Holding her hands close to her collarbone, keeping them elevated above her heart, Marie wanted nothing more than to have Alex wrapped in her arms while Jake held her in his own. She'd fucked up—majorly—but coming out of a near-death experience, her eyes were opened in a whole new way. The perspective she'd been lacking was now front and center.

"Uh, should be there shortly," Don announced from the driver's seat.

Marie looked toward him, smiling weakly. "Okay," she replied, noticing he held his jaw clenched.

Doc Butler's office was on the outskirts of Lordsland, one of the last stops on the road that led to the next town over. Butler was old and had been practicing medicine longer than Marie had been alive. She'd never really liked visiting the old man if it could be helped, often taking Alex to Willow Hill, or a larger city for his routine check-ups.

Now, all things considered—including her current company—she wasn't going to protest the closest option for medical treatment.

He'll probably tell me to take an aspirin and forty-eight hours of bedrest, Marie thought, a soft chuckle slipping from her lips.

Seeing Don's head turn toward her, then a few side-eyed glances in her direction, Marie pressed her lips tightly together.

Clearing her throat, she said, "I can't thank you enough, Don. If you hadn't come along when you did, I... I don't know what would've happened."

Don's head fully turned to face her and they locked eyes—Marie could see the slightest hint of empathy cutting through his cold exterior—before it turned back to the road.

"Glad I could help," he said, grumbling something inaudible under his breath afterward.

The rest of the car ride was uneventful, with no other words passed between them. Doc Butler's office came into view, forcing Marie to break the silence.

"I know I've already put you out so much, but would you be willing to wait long enough for me to get patched up and then give me a ride to Alex's school?" she begrudgingly asked.

Don pulled into the most convenient parking space and killed the engine. Patting his leg as he looked at the other cars there, he said, "Hope the old buzzard isn't too busy. Looks like a full house."

Marie took his non-answer as confirmation and struggled for a moment as she attempted to open the car door with her injured hands. With Don's help, and quick thank you, she exited the car and limped into the office.

She saw a few residents seated in the waiting area and quickly walked to where the receptionist sat.

"I need to see the doctor, please," Marie said, holding up her makeshift-bandaged hands.

The receptionist looked up from the paperwork she'd been filling out, her eyes growing wide, and then looked toward the waiting room.

"Name?" she asked.

"Marie Ward."

"Have you been here before?"

Marie nodded. "Yes, but... it's been awhile."

The harried receptionist searched her files and came up empty. She looked flustered and stared at Marie for a moment. Marie winced as she held her hands higher.

"The doc is busy. If you're not opposed to it, I... I could take a look and see what can be done."

Chewing her lip, Marie nodded slightly and said, "Okay."

Fifteen minutes later, Marie was walking out of Doc Butler's office sterilized, sewn up, and bandaged—with a pocket full of sample painkillers to boot.

"I guess they weren't as busy as they look?" Don asked, tilting his head to Marie's freshly wrapped hands.

After Marie slid into the passenger seat and closed the door, she looked at her hands, testing their dexterity. "So, Butler *was* busy, but his receptionist is a miracle worker."

Don shifted away from her, turning fully to face Marie. "The recep... You're telling me you didn't see the doctor? That his help practiced medicine on you?" He spat the last part and grimaced.

Marie clinched her teeth and remembered why Don was the neighbor no one liked. Choosing her words more carefully, she said, "Good as new," and held up her bandaged hands. "Well, close enough."

Don turned and looked out the windshield, gripping the steering wheel. "In all my years, I've never heard of such... such... malfeasance! Why... it borders on malpractice!" His face reddened and his breathing grew heavy.

Marie's eyes grew wide for a moment and quickly thought of ways to defuse the situation. "So, as we discussed, you said you'd take me to Alex's school when we were done here?"

Slowly nodding, Don started the car. "Right. Alex."

Backing out of the parking space, Marie watched the man's face—his eyes unblinking as they remained locked on the doctor's office, the muscles in his jaw clenching, releasing, then clenching again.

"He really likes you, you know? Alex," Marie lied as they started down the road.

"He's very young," Don replied, curtly.

Marie smiled gently, thinking about her son. "Yeah, he'll be the big one-oh soon. He's getting big."

Lost in thoughts resurfacing after the encounter with Ethan, Marie settled against the door, wondering where Jake was.

The bartender, who Jake now knew as Lilly, had barreled through the door and called for everyone to start barricading every possible entrance and window that led to the outside. Most of the patrons of McGoo's stared at her with apathy, too deep in their glasses to give a shit, no matter what the fuss was about.

"Settle down. And I need topped off," someone said from the back of the bar, belching loudly afterwards.

"Off your asses, you dumbshits. This is serious. There's fucking dead folks everywhere out there," Lilly scolded, throwing the deadbolt on the entrance then moving to the closest table, dragging it to the door and upending it for added protection.

"What the hell is going on, Lil?" Mavid asked from behind Jake.

Lilly stopped mid-step, looking around at everyone. "Dead. People," she reiterated slowly for the well inebriated. "I just had to fight off Daniel Pike to keep him from taking a chunk out of my face."

"Pike? Pike's been dead for nearly twenty years," someone said from the pool table.

"Yeah, I know! And he's very much outside if you'd like to catch up with him," Lilly replied, the patience in her voice waning.

"Nah, I'm good," the guy at the pool table offered back.

Jake stood from his barstool and approached Lilly on wobbly legs. "Whaaa cannn we doo?" His words slurring.

Lilly looked at him for a moment, then at everyone else. "Anyone carrying?"

A clatter rose throughout the bar as every person, aside from Jake, produced a firearm of some sort—including Mavid.

Feeling ill prepared, Jake stumbled back to his barstool to sulk. He watched as Lilly returned to her post behind the bar and started to search through the lower cabinets.

"Ahh!" she exclaimed, rising with a large coffee pot in hand. "If we're going to make it out of here alive, I'm gonna need you fuckers alert."

"I actually aim better with a few in me," Mavid told her, a wide grin on his face.

Lilly lifted a single eyebrow while looking at the man, sliding his glass away and removing it from the bar. "Ain't negotiable, old man. Now, to find that coffee."

"Coffee? How old isit if yaa don't know where tis?" Jake questioned.

"Zip it, sad ass," Lilly scolded just before disappearing back into the cabinet.

Jake looked at Mavid and shrugged, unable to argue with her quip. Propping himself up on the bar, he started to pinch his cheeks, hoping to wake up from the nightmare that had become his life. With financial ruin looming over his head, Marie's revelation of infidelity, and now dead folks walking around outside, his thoughts turned to the single shred of light in his otherwise doom-shrouded mind—Alex.

Alex, Spike, and Rachel had their plan set. Mrs. Nelson was going around the room, talking to children individually about their personal salvation, praying with the ones she felt most in danger of eternal damnation, and was now almost at the end of the first row, which was the farthest away from them as she would be.

Spike suggested he sneak to the front of the class—proclaiming to be the fastest out of the three of them—before unlocking the door and making a break for the main office at the other end of the school where he could alert someone to what was going on in the classroom.

Rachel started to protest, mentioning it was a tie earlier when they raced, but Alex backed Spike, not wanting Rachel to take the risk of getting caught and Mrs. Nelson enacted punishment on her.

"Remember, find Principal Garten, or Ms. Prince, as fast as you can. They have to get us out of here before Mrs. Nelson does something crazy," Alex said, reiterating the plan.

"And tell them everyone is scared. That might get them to come faster," Rachel added.

Spike nodded, checked to see where Mrs. Nelson was at, and slid out of his seat. Alex watched his friend creep alongside the desks in their row, turning so he could keep an eye on their teaching while also watching Spike's progression.

Looking back at Alex, waiting for the signal, Spike waited before leaving the safety of cover. Alex waved, indicating it was safe to go. Spike took four long strides, while staying crouched, and disappeared behind Mrs. Nelson's desk. He heard Rachel groan behind him and went to motion for her to stay quiet, but was shocked when she grabbed his hand and held it—squeezing it tightly.

Not wanting to risk drawing attention, Alex pushed the thought of his crush holding his hand away from the forefront of his mind and looked forward to see Spike's head pop up from behind the desk. With a quick glance at Mrs. Nelson—who had her head bowed in prayer—Alex motioned for him to go. He watched as Spike moved swiftly and silently, impressed by the boy's stealth capabilities, until he reached the door that led to the hallway.

The nervousness on Spike's face was plain as day to Alex, who was sitting all the way across the room, and he couldn't blame him. He still felt the overwhelming need to be home with his parents, but looking back, first at their interlocked hands, then up to Rachel's face, Alex guessed things could be a lot worse, all things considered.

An audible click sounded through the otherwise quiet room, and Alex's head quickly turned to see Spike standing at the door, looking like a deer in headlights.

"Blasphemous! Sinner!" Mrs. Nelson bellowed as she stood and pointed at Spike.

Without thinking, Alex yelled, "Go!" to his friend, drawing the attention of everyone in the room to him for a moment.

As if coming out of hypnosis, Spike shook his head before throwing open the door and disappearing into the corridor. Mrs. Nelson charged after him, yelling words in some kind of language Alex had never heard, also disappearing into the hallway.

The quiet classroom erupted into a raucous roar, students whooping and hollering, until they saw Mrs. Nelson re-entering the room, slamming the door shut behind her.

"Naughty, naughty," she croaked, rolling her head around on her shoulders. "I think I've been going about this all wrong, children." Her eyes looked overtop the others, locking on Alex. "Spare the rod, spoil the child."

Chapter Five

Nearly back from her dentist appointment in Willow Hill, Megan smiled at herself in the rearview mirror, checking out her new braces. She'd always been self-conscious of her teeth, often refusing to smile in pictures, but since splitting up with her ex-boyfriend a few months ago, she was making it a point to address all of her insecurities.

Bobby had done a number on her self-esteem during their time together. Intrusive thoughts often reared their ugly head when she was at her lowest. But since the break-up, and a few prospects of some good times to be had, Megan felt she was finally on track and ready to reintroduce herself to the world.

Approaching a stoplight that would lead her to the main drag in Lordsland, she couldn't help doing another quick glance in the mirror, admiring the bright, shiny metal attached to her rich, white teeth. Pulling her eyes away from her reflection, Megan's attention was drawn to something nearby.

Checking the light and seeing it was still red, Megan glanced over and saw a man standing on the curb. His clothes were ripped and tattered, and he looked like he hadn't bathed in years. She looked forward again, hoping the stranger wouldn't approach, begging for money or something.

Relief flooded in as the light turned green and she drove away, checking the side-mirror to see the man looking off into the sky. Back in the groove of driving, Megan's thoughts returned to her plans for the upcoming weekend, and Ethan.

As she approached the next stoplight, she could see three more strangers standing close to the road.

"Come on, come on, come on..." she mumbled, praying the light remained green. "Shit!"

Coming to a stop at the light—now red—she noticed the three loiters were just as bedraggled as the last guy. Hoping vagrancy wasn't becoming a normalcy in Lordsland, Megan kept her eyes forward, willing the light to change as fast as possible.

A shadow cast from her left and she looked to see that one of the bums had walked up to her window. Sighing, she reached into her purse and pulled out a five-dollar bill while rolling down the driver's side window.

"Here, I hope this hel—" Megan started to say but jerked when something sharp bit into her hand. "Motherfucker!" she cried.

Pulling her hand back into the car, she saw a large chunk of flesh was missing. Whimpering at the sight of her own blood, Megan quickly looked to see the stranger was greedily chewing on a piece of her hand. Wheezing and ragged breaths accompanied the chewing noises when she started to shriek.

The other vagrants that had assembled near the stoplight were now bumping into and climbing on top of Megan's car, moaning as they pounded on the metal and glass that kept her separated from them. Her foot punched the accelerator and the car shot forward, scattering the would-be assailants in her wake.

Blood poured from the missing portion of her skin, running down the steering wheel and splashing into her lap. The injured hand was doing more harm than good, hindering Megan's ability to grasp the wheel properly due to the slick blood.

Speeding down Main Street, more homeless people littered the road, turning toward her as she came near. As she passed one at high speed, she thought the person was missing their arm and craned around to do a double take.

"What the fuck is going on?" she uttered as she turned back—and then gasped.

Half a dozen people were standing directly in front of her. Megan quickly shifted her foot to the brake pedal and attempted to swerve around the group, but couldn't keep a hold on the blood-slicked steering wheel. Tires screeched as she plowed through them, body parts flying off in all directions.

A brick façade filled the windshield before everything went black.

A loud crash outside made Barb jump, nearly falling out of her chair as she did. She rose to her feet, remembering to grab the gun Shipley had given her, before moving to the entrance. Peering through the blinds, Barb saw a car had crashed into the barbershop across the street, steam billowing out from the crumpled hood.

Pulling the door open, she rushed across the road and looked in the car, seeing the driver was the only passenger. Before opening the driver's door, she looked down Main Street and saw bodies littered the pavement.

"Oh, sweet Jesus," she said.

Regretting leaving the handheld radio in the station—unable to call for assistance—Barb opened the door, wincing at the groan it made, and knelt down. The airbag had gone off on impact, and the driver—a girl, as best she could tell—had their face buried in the inflated deflated material.

"Can you hear me? Are you with me?" Barb asked and then felt for a pulse. "Still alive."

Shifting the revolver to her left hand, Barb reached in and tried to shift the driver back in their seat from being slumped against the wheel. Something was catching, preventing the girl from being moved.

Knowing she should go back into the station and radio the sheriff, Barb, instead, placed the revolver on the sidewalk and used both hands to hold the driver's head steady as she worked to free it from the steering wheel.

Finally able to move the driver freely, Barb eased the person back into the seat and shifted away suddenly, stumbling and then falling on her ass. The driver's face was covered in blood, and she could see jagged pieces of metal poking out through her lips at odd angles.

Before Barb could think of what to do next, she heard someone approaching from the road. Gaining her feet as quickly as she could, she saw something that was only in the movies—a corpse with hollowed out eyes was making its way toward her.

Remembering the revolver on the ground, Barb bent and picked it up.

"Stop!" she commanded. "Not another step!"

The putrid corpse continued its progress, pieces of it sloughing off, and she took aim. Her finger smoothly squeezing the trigger, the shot was surprisingly loud to her, but the result was not. She watched as the body fell to the ground, now missing a large portion of its head.

Scanning the street, Barb saw a few she originally thought to be bystanders of a car accident were now crawling over the pavement.

A million scenarios raced through her mind, and she knew she had to act fast. Ducking quickly into the car, she tried to rouse the driver, but was still unable to.

"Cheese and crackers," she moaned, and then closed the driver's door.

Stepping away from the car, Barb took aim at the closest corpse while heading back to the station and pulled the trigger, dropping it in a flash. Remembering everything Shipley had taught her during their trips to the range, she kept both eyes open, staying aware of her surroundings.

Halfway across the street, her senses were heightened to the point of stressing her out. Every sight, sound, and smell worked against her now, forcing false perceptions into her already overtaxed mind.

The stench of rotting flesh was overwhelming, and more and more folks she knew for a fact were well past their expiration date were bearing down on her.

Barb took two quick shots at Judi Zeiders and Joe Lerner, leaving them sprawled in the middle of the road, sans their heads.

Ten yards away from the front entrance, she took another perfect shot at Erin Koplin, sending head shrapnel into the ones following close behind.

Risking it, she turned her back to the encroaching corpses and trotted as fast as her knees would allow until she was safely inside the police station.

Taking a deep breath, Barb walked over to the radio on her desk, and keyed the mic. "Sheriff, you there?" She waited a moment for Shipley to reply and then keyed the mic again. "Shipley, you got a copy?"

Normally Barb wouldn't be so informal on the police band, but the situation made her throw caution to the wind. Scratching the side of her head with the hot barrel of the revolver, she started to tap her foot as she waited.

"Go ahead, Barb," Shipley finally answered, his tone harried.

Pausing a moment to gather her thoughts, Barb took another deep breath. "We have a bit of a situation here at the station, Sheriff. I don't know what's going on out there... but I had to shoot someone. Well, a few someones. And there's been a vehicle accident outside the station and a Jane Doe is unconscious inside. I can not get her out on my own."

"Jeeeezus, Barb!" Shipley came back with. "I'm over next to Oak Cabins. It'll take me a bit to get back there. Any word from Jon or Brent?"

Barb shook her head before answering. "No, nothing. There's people outside in the street. They look... dead. But, Sheriff... they're still moving around."

A long pause of silence passed over the radio before the sheriff replied. "Barb, are you okay? Did you hit your head or something?"

Rolling her eyes, she replied, "No, I'm perfectly fine. So cut the bull-hockey. I'm telling you how it is."

As Shipley keyed up his mic to talk, Barb could hear the sirens wailing in the background. "Stay put and don't try to do anything until I get there. I mean it, Barb. Stay in the station."

Blowing a raspberry with her lips, Barb said, "Okay, I will."

"On my way," was all Shipley voiced over the engine roar and siren cry.

Barb walked over to the front entrance and looked out through the blinds. The few things she saw crawling on the ground were starting to crowd the front of the station. More unnerving, at least to her, were the ones she didn't remember being out on the street now walking around aimlessly, as if on a leisurely stroll through town.

Though her grip was firm enough to ensure its readiness, should the call to action arise, the revolver clattered to the floor as Barb raised her hands to cover her mouth in shock. Walking down the road, twenty feet from where she stood, was her son—who had died in Iraq over ten years ago and had been buried in Pleasant Ridge Cemetery when his body had been shipped back to the states. He was still wearing the uniform he'd been buried in.

Without realizing, Barb's hand reached for the door.

Shipley had driven out to the edge of town and planned to work his way through various neighborhoods to access any damage from the storm. He had a list of things to address when he got back to the station, calling in tree removal services and such, and was nearing Pleasant Ridge Cemetery when Barb broke radio silence.

The sheriff listened as his secretary talked craziness across the police band. *Did she really shoot someone?* he wondered. And after doing a quick U-turn just short of the road that led up to the cemetery, Shipley hit the switches for the lights and siren and told Barb to stay put.

A quick calculation in his head told him he could be back at the station in ten minutes if nothing slowed him down along the way. Traffic around town had been surprisingly light during his initial drive through—*damn near a ghost town* he'd said to himself—especially for a weekday.

Moving the thought to the back of his mind, Shipley raced past Doc Butler's office, seeing a few sickly looking folks standing in the parking lot. Fall usually brought early, on-set sickness to a lot of residents of Lordsland with the bi-polar weather patterns. Hot and muggy one day, cold and rainy the next, and sometime early winter snows reared their ugly head when mother nature was feeling really moody.

Coming to an intersection, the sheriff eased off the accelerator a bit, checking to see if the coast was clear, before hammering it to the floor again. His cruiser groaned as it raced down the street. Coming around a curve that would put him on a straight shot to the police station, Shipley saw a few cars stopped in the middle of the road, driver's doors open, but no drivers in sight.

"Jon, Brent, where are you currently located?" he called into the mic. Static was the only reply he received. "Goddamnit, where the fuck are those two?"

Anger rising at his absentee deputies, Shipley pushed the cruiser to its limits, barreling through the next intersection without a second glance for any oncoming traffic. The police station was fast approaching and he could see the wrecked vehicle sitting on the sidewalk, along with a group of onlookers.

Laying on the horn to clear the way, the sheriff slowed his car and rolled down the window. "Out of the road," he yelled, beeping twice to get his point across.

The group was either so enraptured by the accident that they didn't hear him, or they simply didn't care. Growling, Shipley threw the shifter into park and got out.

"Hey, I said clear the ro—"

The sheriff stopped cold in his tracks when he saw the closest person from the crowd. His head shook in disbelief from what his eyes were seeing. Before him stood the former sheriff, George Slaughter, who had died suddenly from a botched appendectomy two years ago. Two years in the grave had been unkind to old George, in Shipley's quick assessment.

Backing away from the approaching dead man, he was jolted to his senses when the ungiving firmness of the police cruiser halted his retreat. Remembering himself, Shipley drew his sidearm from its holster in one quick, fluid motion.

"S-stay right there, George. Just stay t-there," he warned, taking aim.

The corpse of George Slaughter continued without hesitation, its footsteps labored. Wincing from the thought of what he had to do, Shipley said, "I'm s-sorry, George."

The report from the service pistol rang out down Main Street, finally drawing the attention of the others. A weak cry slipped from the sheriff's mouth as they all turned to face him; he recognized every one of their faces instantly.

Tommy Frei had died during a drunk driving accident years ago. Natasha Mazer succumbed to a long battle with cancer earlier in the spring. Cameron Mueller was killed during a freak hunting accident when Shipley was just a kid—the man's eyeless skull boring into him with an unnatural hatred that made the sheriff shiver.

Everyone in the streets had been a person Shipley knew, whether in passing or on a personal level. And every person on the street, walking around or looking in his direction, he knew was now dead. Turning to get back in his car, the sheriff's reflexes were sharp, but not sharp enough as a hand reached out and raked its fingernails across his face.

He jerked away and turned to see his secretary walking toward him, a growl issuing from her mouth he never knew she was capable of.

"Baaarb?" Shipley moaned as he back-stepped toward the police station. "No, Barb... not you. NOT YOU!"

More and more townsfolk were bearing down on him and all he could think about was Barb—now missing a large portion of her neck and a fresh coat of blood covering her clothes—as he backed away from the undead mob.

"Please, Barb, say something!" Shipley cried, tears welling in his eyes.

From his periphery, the sheriff saw someone approaching from the left and looked to see Patrick Miller—heart attack in a movie theater while watching a superhero film—reaching for him with rotting, skeletal fingers. Hip firing, Shipley took out one of the dead man's kneecaps, causing its body to crumple to the ground.

With one last fleeting look at Barb, Shipley turned away from the advancing deceased and raced for the entrance of the police station. Tucking his shoulder, he burst through the door and sent something skidding across the floor and out of sight. Too worried to care what it was, he quickly turned and locked the door just as one of dead residents of Lordsland came crashing against it.

Backing away and aiming, waiting for his would-be assailants to knock the door down, Shipley watched in surprise as, one by one, they slowly seemed to lose interest in their pursuit and started to peel away, going their separate ways.

His attention was grabbed from movement in the distance as the wrecked vehicle's door opened up. A young girl, by his estimates, got out and stood next to the car. She looked confused and had to keep one hand braced on the door to keep herself upright. Shipley stepped closer to the door, wanting nothing more than to race out there and grab her, but knew the second he did so, the dead would swarm him.

Squinting, the sheriff saw her face was covered in blood from her nose down, and had spread over the front of her shirt, much the same as Barb's had been. Sighing deeply at his lack of usefulness, Shipley gripped his sidearm tighter as he watched the girl walk on unsteady legs—how a fawn would when learning to walk—moving to the closest person that was wandering the street.

A scream rang out that curdled the sheriff's blood. It was garbled, but no less horrifying in its delivery. The scream had an adverse effect in drawing attention to the girl she didn't know she didn't want. He watched her make it three steps before the first walking corpse dragged her to the pavement.

Placing a hand on the lock, ready to throw it and race outside, Shipley backed away when he saw Barb step up to the window of the door. The young girl's muffled cries for help play as the soundtrack while Sheriff Dan Shipley and his now dead lover stared at one another. His eyes filled with pain, Barb's filled with hunger.

Chapter Six

Jake Ward, along with the patrons of McGoo's, was doing his best to sober up through copious amounts of shitty coffee and plans of their escape. The more the alcohol's effect waned on Jake, the more he realized just how pungent an odor the bar held.

"Listen up, everyone!" Lilly said, snapping her fingers. "I'm going to go over this one more time. So pull your heads out your asses or it'll be your *asses* that pay the price."
Everyone gathered around the bar, a few of them grumbling about how terrible the coffee was, or voicing their displeasure about a woman taking the lead over their survival.

"Can it, Hank. I've had enough of your lip already," Lilly chastised.

Jake saw the man hang his head and shuffle away from the bar quietly.

"Now, as we've gone over half a dozen times already, we need to stay in a tight group—no gaps. That's what keeps us protected on all sides. We stay together and move as one until we get to... what's your name again?" she asked, pointing to a guy with a mullet.

"Adkins," he replied.

"Right, Adkins' truck. We should all be able to fit in the cab and bed and get the fuck outta Dodge. I CANNOT STRESS THIS ENOUGH. If we don't stay together, these dead sumbitches will pick us off, one by one, no problem. Strength in numbers, fellas." Lilly threw her hands on her hips to accentuate her point.

"Okay, Okay... I follow you, but what makes you such a god-damned expert on alpaca-lip-tick survival tactics, hmm?" Hank had found his courage again, stepping back up to the bar, causing a few of the others to nod to his question.

Jake watched from his stool as Lilly's demeanor changed in an instant. Her arms fell slack at her sides as her eyes narrowed in on him. Taking a sip of the bitter coffee, Jake felt as though he was watching a showdown from an old western movie. Before he could register what happened, Hank barked out in shock and pain as Lilly's fist met with his nose.

Mavid whooped out in surprise and started laughing as the crowd cleared, allowing Hank to fall flat on his back, blood running over his face from the broken nose he was now nursing. Lilly walked around the bar, the others giving her a wide berth as she stood over the injured man, bending to look him in the eyes.

"Because I play a shit-ton of video games, asshole!" she answered, drawing back again and watching Hank flinch away in fear.

Returning to her position behind the bar, Lilly addressed them all, once again. "Now, if everyone is done fucking around, I would like to get out of here."

A half-hearted cheer rose from everyone, Jake included, and he looked over at Mavid. "I've never shot one of these things before," he told the old timer.

"Kid, it's easy. Just point and pull the trigger. The gun does the rest." Mavid gave him a reassuring smile and checked his own gun one last time.

Jake looked down at the firearm Lilly had loaned him with the promise of him returning it once they knew they were in the clear. It felt heavy in his hand, and weighed more heavily on his mind when he asked himself if he could really shoot another person with it. When he'd voiced his concern to the bartender and his new friend, they both assured him that things waiting outside were no longer living, therefore no longer human.

When Jake first looked out the window and saw the corpses of the dead residents—most of whom had been buried long before he and his family had moved into town—he thought he was on a movie set that had enlisted Hollywood's top special effects team. But after watching dilapidated corpses walking around outside for a few minutes—a few bumping into one another, causing rotted body parts to break loose and fall to the ground—he knew it was all real, and instantly thought of getting back to Marie and Alex.

Steeling his nerves, Jake ejected the gun's magazine—just as Lilly had shown him—and saw it was still fully loaded from his last check. Picking up his cup of coffee from the bar and tossing the last few mouthfuls back and swallowing it down in one gulp, Jake stood from his stool and nodded to Mavid.

Looking over at Lilly, he saw a playful grin on the woman's face. She winked at him before saying, "Let's do this shit."

The reaction from the crowd this time was more boisterous than the previous one.

Leading the pack, Lilly turned to address them all one last time and reiterate the simple plan. "Stay together. Get to Adkins' truck. Blue Ford."

"Azure sky blue Ford F-150 extended crew cab," Adkins corrected, beaming with pride.

"Nice," someone said from the back of the group.

Lilly stared at him for a moment. "Right."

Jake took a deep breath when he saw Lilly roll her eyes and turn away to face the door. He held the gun in one hand, and an old broken mop handle in the other. Part of their planning had been to arm everyone as best they could with what they had to work with. Everyone was armed with at least one firearm—some even duel-wielding—and various forms of clubs or shields to protect themselves from being attacked.

As he breathed out slowly, Lilly threw the door open, the sun temporarily blinding Jake and the other from its brightness. Trampling one another as they all funneled through the bottleneck of the entrance, Jake held his gun hand over his eyes as they adjusted to the blast of natural light.

He was being pushed around from all sides. By the time he was able to look around the parking lot, Lilly had already encountered one of the dead that had been hanging around the door.

Pulling the sharpened pool cue from the pierced skull, she yelled for everyone to keep moving. Jake kept pace with her, huddling close but still trying not to crowd her in case she needed to spring into action. Adkins' truck was parked at the very end of the lot, positioned in a way so no one else could pull in close to it and risk a door ding.

Three walking, human husks came stutter-stepping from around the corner. Adkins yelped in surprise, Mavid growled, Jake stopped walking for a moment before pushing forward, and Lilly told them to keep moving.

She steered the mobile phalanx toward the road, moving away from the bar, and balked when she saw another small group of zombies huddled around the truck.

"Why the fuck are they all standing around your truck for?" Lilly asked harshly.

"Uh, well, I guess they're trying to get Cici," Adkins admitted, the tone of his voice growing higher in pitch.

"Cici?" Mavid asked, tripping over his own feet before Jake caught and corrected him.

"I-it's my dog. A chihuahua," Adkins said.

Lilly stopped on a dime, turned—ignoring their current predicament—and squinted at the man. "Are you telling me you had your dog locked up in that truck all morning while you were inside drinkin'?"

Before he could begin to answer, she lunged at the man, performing an encore with his nose as she did Hank, sending him staggering back.

"Now's not the time. We got bigger fish to fry," Mavid interjected, pointing at another group of corpses emerging from the woods that ran along the road opposite the bar.

"This isn't over, motherfucker," Lilly threatened. "Move!"

Jake looked back as the group moved on, seeing Adkins collect himself, wiping fresh blood from face, and tears from his eyes. Quickly, the man's face changed from pain to hurt to anger. Raising the battered trash can lid over his head, Adkins screamed and charged at them like a bull.

"Look out!" Jake yelled, dragging Mavid out of the man's path.

Adkins bowled through the first few at the back of the group, knocking them to the ground, and continued on toward Lilly. She had spun around at Jake's warning and deftly side-stepped the angry man's rush. Adkins' momentum worked against him and he tripped over the bartender's outstretched foot—sending him to the ground.

Without a second thought, she aimed and put a 9mm slug into his thigh. The shot rang as Adkins howled in pain. Lilly quickly stepped over him, first grabbing the gun laying beside him on the road, then fishing a set of keys from his pocket. The gunshot worked as a party favor, drawing the attention of every dead thing within a hundred yard radius, hastening their pursuit—including the ones that were after Cici.

"Get to the truck!" one of the others yelled just as a set of cold, dead hands dragged him to the ground.

The group scattered as the deceased risen of Lordsland descended on them. Shots rang out from all directions. Jake took Mavid by the arm—abandoning his mop handle—and started leading him to the F-150.

Lilly was already there, opening the driver's door, by the time they got close enough to hear Cici's yips. Opening the door, Jake backed away as Mavid climbed in and saw one of the undead climbing out of the truck's bed.

"Oh shit!" he yelled as it tumbled out and landed on him.

Crashing to the ground, Jake dropped his gun as he put his hands up to protect himself. Despite being dead, the corpse still had heft, and it took all the strength he had to keep the snapping maw from biting into his face. Fetid, stinking breath filled his nose. The more he struggled against the dead thing, the more strain it was on his arms. Jake felt himself losing against the relentless creature that was inching closer and closer.

Ready to scream and give in, Jake saw something fast move into his field of vision, and the zombie's head flew away from its body. Looking up, he saw Lilly had punted it away and was now looking around for another would-be, undead assassin.

"Quit fucking around and git in the truck," she said, leaving him to push away the headless body and get to his feet.

Grabbing the gun from the ground, Jake quickly looked around the parking lot to see everyone engaged in their own personal battles between life and literal death, and then jumped into the seat behind Mavid—who was riding shotgun—before slamming the door shut behind him. Lilly got in and turned the key in the ignition; the truck roared to life.

"Are you just going to leave them behind?" Jake asked, craning his head around to see more and more zombies joining the fight.

Looking back from the driver's seat, Lilly said, "Do you want to go out there and give them a hand?"

Staying silent, Jake shook his head in shame. Something wet touched his hand and he jerked away, only to find a small dog sitting next to him, wagging its tail.

"Cici, I presume?" Jake said.

"Cici," Lilly confirmed as she shifted the Ford into drive. "Where to?"

"Lordsland Middle," Jake said without hesitation.

The truck peeled out of the parking lot and away from the screams.

Mrs. Nelson stood at the head of the classroom, stone-faced and solemn. After Spike's exodus, the students had erupted in cries of wanting to leave, wanting to go home. None had been more vocal than Marty Davis, who had gone so far as to get in Mrs. Nelson's face—drawing gasps from most of the students—demanding she unlock the door and let them leave.

Alex watched in complete and utter dismay as Mrs. Nelson quickly struck out, catching Marty in the throat with her hand, causing the boy to fall to his knees. Mrs. Nelson called for two of the bigger boys in class to restrain the one at her feet who was struggling to suck in air.

After they got Marty back to his feet, Mrs. Nelson retrieved a bundle of yarn from the supply cabinet the students used for art projects. Hands restrained in front of him, Marty was forced to his knees, facing the rest of the class as Mrs. Nelson addressed them.

"I wasn't sure which of you to choose for salvation first, but the divine grace of God has given us our first lamb. Young Marty here, though wild and untamed in our eyes, shall be the first of us to meet the Lord on high, and His everlasting grace of forgiveness."
Alex looked back at Rachel, raising his eyebrows, and she returned his questioning look with her own frightened reaction in the form of a shrug, biting her bottom lip.

Finally able to speak, Marty protested his imprisonment. "Let me go, you crazy old bitch!"

Another collective gasp sounded from the students while Mrs. Nelson's face remained placid. Quietly, she walked behind her desk, jerking one of the drawers open so harshly, it came free from the desk and its contents spilled onto the floor. Bending to retrieve a scarf she kept there, Mrs. Nelson returned to the boy and gagged him with it.

Motioning with her head for the two bigger boys to come close, Mrs. Nelson whispered something to them that caused Marty's eyes to grow wide. Alex watched as one of the boys stepped away from the teacher, going to the door of the classroom, while the other took Mrs. Nelson's position behind Marty as she made her way to the windows.

"The time for purification has come. Bring him," Mrs. Nelson said to the boy guarding Marty.

Pulling him to his feet, the bigger boy shoved him forward, keeping in step with him as they walked between the rows of students. Marty looked and locked eyes with Alex for a brief moment, the fear Alex saw in them shook him to his core.

While all attention was on the bound boy, everyone failed to notice Mrs. Nelson had opened one of the windows at the back of the classroom until Rachel spoke.

"Oh my god!"

Alex spun around in his seat and looked, his heart leaping into his throat. A breeze began to filter into the room, carrying with it the stench of decades worth of grave rot.

"Ew, it stinks," one of the other students commented.

When Marty saw where he was being led, he stopped and attempted to backpedal, but was met with the resistance of the bigger boy behind him. Muffled pleas could be heard through the gag, indistinct cries.

As they reached their teacher, Marty was struggling to get away, but was outmatched by Mrs. Nelson's enlisted disciple in height and weight.

Watching from his seat, Alex felt he should be doing something, anything to help his fellow classmate, but didn't know what he could do to prevent what was about to happen—or become next in line for the same fate.

"This is insane," Alex said, low enough for only Rachel to hear.

She didn't speak a reply, but Alex saw tears in her eyes, a few streaming down her cheeks, when she turned toward him before looking back to the windows.

"Martin Davis, I commit you, body and soul, to serve a far greater purpose than you could possibly comprehend. May your light shine forever more, and be a beacon to the lost souls still wandering this miserable, self-indulgent existence."

With a curt nod, she and the bigger kid each grabbed one of Marty's arms and started dragging him closer to the open window. Bucking against them, the boy stood no chance of saving himself while currently being restrained. Other kids in the classroom were now standing, watching the madness unfold before them in complete awe, a few shedding silent tears, including Alex, who couldn't believe what he was seeing.

At the window, Mrs. Nelson grabbed the back of Marty's pants and yelled, "Be free, child!" before hoisting him up with the help of the student, sending him out into the playground area. The teacher wasted no time in closing the window, preventing Marty from attempting to get back inside.

She turned to the class, a crazed smile spreading across her face, and said, "Come, watch."

One by one, the other kids took a spot near the windows, watching to see what happened next. Alex and Rachel held back from having a front row seat, opting to huddle together in a corner as far away from Mrs. Nelson as they could get. Despite that, Alex still watched out of morbid curiosity.

Marty was on his feet now, and had taken the gag out, looking around as if trying to figure out which route to take. The playground was littered with zombies, and there was no clear path to safety from what Alex could see. Darting forward, Marty narrowly escaped one of the undead that crawled out from under one of shrubs next to the building. The attention of the other corpses was drawn to the boy by something unperceivable by everyone in the classroom. All at once, the hoard was bearing down on him from every side.

"No, no, no," a girl next to Mrs. Nelson said, receiving a stern look from the teacher.

Marty stood still for a moment, again looking around, waiting for a single opportunity to make his move. Alex could see the boy was working to loosen the yarn that was binding his hands. Lost in concentrated effort, Marty didn't see the two dead coming up behind him.

"Someone warn him!" Rachel barked, drawing the attention of most of the class, including Mrs. Nelson, whose eyes narrowed at the girl.

"Oh my god, look!" the bigger kid who'd helped exile Marty said, pointing.

Everyone witnessed as Marty was surprised from behind, tripping when he tried to back away. A dogpile of ravenous corpses fell on the boy—his screams ringing out over the playground, quickly tapering off into the sound of the ripping and tearing into his flesh, pulling away chunks with their chomping mouths and bony fingers.

Rachel turned away, sobbing, as did most of the other students. Alex hung his head next to hers, putting his arm around her shoulders as her body shook with silent sobs.

"He is in a better place. Students, please take your seat," Mrs. Nelson said, the tone of voice holding an odd, serene timbre.

No one protested, whether out of fear or apathy was anyone's guess. Making sure she made it to her seat, Alex patted Rachel's back reassuringly before sliding into his own chair.

Mrs. Nelson walked to the front of the classroom, perching in front of the chalkboard.

"Let us pray, children, and see which soul is next to be freed. The divine spirit will guide us all."

Spike had bolted from the classroom, Mrs. Nelson hot on his heels yelling gibberish at him. Feeling he had made it a safe enough distance, he quickly turned, threw up both middle fingers, relishing the look of disgust on her face, and then continued on. As he raced down the corridor, the floor had been newly waxed, which affected the grip of his shoes, but Spike was able to maintain speed, correcting his footing when needed.

As he passed by other classrooms, he could see the doors to them had remained open, and kids inside were all staring out the windows—teachers included. A few students also lingered in the hallway, gawking at him as he sped past.

Approaching the front office, Spike skidded a few times as he tried to curb his momentum. There were adults buzzing in and out of the doors, some who looked to be parents were asking the school's staff to get their kid from class so they could take them home.

Stepping up the secretary's desk, Spike bounced from heel to toe as Mrs. Barnswood held up her hand as she finished the call she was on.

"Yes. Yes, I understand something strange is going on around town, Mr. Davis, but I can assure you we are taking this very seriously. All students are safe and accounted for, in their homerooms. No, I haven't spoken with his teacher personally, but I'm sure Marty is fine. Yes, the buses will be here within the hour for early dismissal. Okay, and you as well, Mr. Davis." Mrs. Barnswood hung up the phone and looked at Spike with tired eyes.

"Yes, Mr. Kneeland?" she asked.

Spike was about to lay out everything that was going on in Mrs. Nelson's room when another parent came into the office from outside, requesting to pick up their child.

"I need someone to go down to Mrs. Nelson's room. She's locked everyone inside," he said, but was drowned out by the irate parent.

Rubbing the center of her forehead, Mrs. Barnswood told Spike to have a seat while she attended to the parent, promising to get back with him as soon as possible. Hanging his head in defeat, Spike settled into one of the chairs at the other side of the office, watching the parent demanding to pick up their kid.

Looking, he saw another parent get in line behind the current one being attended to, and then another joined the que shortly after.

Leaning his head back against the wall, he waited, wondering who else he could ask for help.

As they were pulling up to the front of the school, both Marie and Don expressed their surprise at how many cars were parked outside.

"What is this malarky all about?" Don asked.

Without answering, Marie undid her seatbelt and opened the car door. Jumping out, just before closing the door, she turned and said, "I'll be right back. Me and Alex. Hang tight."

She closed the door to whatever Don was saying, no doubt about him not being their keeper, or something along those lines.

She headed for the front entrance and saw there was a line already formed leading into the office where she needed to go. As Marie entered the school, she paused briefly at the line, then bypassed it, knowing where to go to retrieve Alex from class.

Heading down the east wing, kids' excited shouts drew her attention and she stopped in one of the classroom doorways to see what was going on. Everyone was gathered at the windows, watching something unfold on the playground. Going to her tippy-toes to see over their heads, Marie could just make out someone outside, running around, being chased by what looked to be grown-ups.

The class she was watching with gave a collective gasp—including herself—as they watched the boy lose his footing and fall to the ground, followed by the things that were chasing him. The teacher of the class broke away from on-lookers and raced toward Marie, tears wetting her cheeks. Marie stepped aside as she watched the teacher walk briskly toward the office.

A chill racing up her spine, Marie turned and moved down the hallway, picking up her pace the more she thought about what they'd just witnessed.

Approaching Alex's homeroom, she noticed it was the only door in the corridor that was closed.

Reaching to turn the handle, Marie found the door was locked. Peering through the small window, she saw Mrs. Nelson was standing at the front of the class, a girl kneeling in front of her.

Marie knocked on the door, her hand twinging in pain as she did. "Hey, I need to get my son," she said through the glass.

Mrs. Nelson turned and looked at her, sneering, before turning back to the class. Toward the back, she and Alex locked eyes briefly, and he jumped from his seat, racing for the door. Marie's son was intercepted by another student, forcing Alex to sit back down at his desk.

"Open the door," Marie said louder, shaking the door handle as she did.

Mrs. Nelson ignored the request, continuing to do whatever it was she was doing, spreading her arms out and raising them. Marie saw the girl at Mrs. Nelson's feet, crying, and the look of fear on the student's faces sent off an alarm bell in her mind.

Saying something Marie couldn't hear, all heads turned to the windows, where the boy that had grabbed Alex was now opening one of them. Mrs. Nelson reached and pulled the girl on the floor to her feet. Thinking of the boy on the playground moments earlier, Marie put two and two together and started beating and kicking the door as hard as she could.

"Hey!" someone said from behind.

Spike left the office after it was clear no one there would be able to help him any time soon. His first thought was to go back to class and try and take out Mrs. Nelson, but knew there was a chance he'd fail and suffer for his mistake. The second idea that struck him was to find a janitor, or, at the very least, the janitor's closet and see if there was something in there that might help level the playing field and free the captive students.

Racing off toward the cafeteria, Spike recalled—vaguely—seeing a storage closet close to it. The large lunchroom was the closest part of the school to the playground, and when students were done eating, they exited out the back to go outside and play.

Pulling up short of the door that led inside to the cafeteria, Spike looked through the narrow window, seeing a few of the dead things walking around.

"Ugh, these assholes are everywhere," he said with disgust.

Looking around the small entranceway, Spike saw exactly what he was looking for in the form of a door with a placard that read

"Janitorial." Pulling the door open, the dark space didn't hold any hidden treasures to vanquish great foes like in his favorite video games, but there was an old mop and bucket. Grabbing the mop, Spike took off back to his homeroom.

Halfway there, a glass panel set in the wall drew his attention.

"Oh. Yes," Spike said, nodding his head.

Using the mop handle, he broke the glass and pulled out the fire ax that was mounted behind it. Discarding the mop in lieu of the upgrade, Spike braced it with both hands and continued down the corridor. Though passing by a few people, no one asked why he was toting an ax around.

Nearing the classroom, he saw someone pounding on the door, begging to be let in.

"Hey," Spike said.

A woman turned to look at him and he recognized Alex's mom right away. "Oh my god, Spike... How did you get out? What's going on in there? Why are you carrying an ax around?" Marie asked, hitting him with a barrage of questions.

Spike looked down at the ax in his hands and then back up at her and shook his head. "No time to explain all that. Mrs. Nelson went nuts! We need to rescue everybody."

Marie didn't hesitate as she reached for the ax, Spike seeing her grimace when she tried to grip it.

"My hands... I don't think I can. Can you?" she said.

Motioning with his head for her to step aside, Spike tightened his hands around the handle and swung the ax at the door. The head glanced off the hardwood, forcing him to jump back to avoid being hit.

"Here, let me do it," someone said from behind Spike and Marie.

Jake sat anxiously in the back of the F-150, petting Cici in an attempt to calm his nerves. The closer they drew to the school, the more proliferated Lordsland seemed to be with dead residents. It sparked a conversation between him, Mavid, and Lilly when they saw Anita Donavan standing over a dead paramedic, gore covering her face as she dove back in to feast on the first responder's entrails.

"I know for a fact Anita was alive and well yesterday. She always goes out to buy two lottery tickets on Tuesday and I ran into her at the Gas 'N Go last night. Before the storm hit, that is," Mavid explained.

"Yeah, I've definitely seen some folks that I thought were still kickin'. They *are* still kickin', but they looked a little... dead to me now. Something fucky is going on around here." Lilly looked in the rear view and she and Jake's eyes met until hers shifted back to the road.

Mavid scoffed. "No shit. What clued you in on that? The murderous corpses walking around? Or the fact I ain't had a drink in over an hour?"

Jake opted to let the two in the front banter while his mind was occupied with worst case scenarios of what might be happening to Alex and Marie. The scenarios were quite vivid, but in his line of work, being a writer meant he had to think of the craziest things imaginable, and then amp those up to ten if he wanted it to be memorable for his readers. Being lost in his own thoughts was counterproductive though, and Jake tried to clear his mind while giving Cici some attention.

"Jake? Did you hear me, Jake?" Lilly asked.

Mavid turned in his seat and looked at him, concerned.

"What was it?" Jake asked. "I got lost for a moment there."

"I said we should be at the school soon. Another couple of miles or so."

Nodding, Jake said, "Okay."

He saw Lilly and Mavid exchange a quick look. Cici had settled in, snuggling up beside Jake's leg, content with his petting and the rocking motion of the truck. Closing his eyes as he continued to stroke the little dog's fur, Jake still didn't know what he was supposed to do about his Marie situation. Whether he wanted to admit it or not, he couldn't help but still love her. Everything he did was to create a better life for her and Alex.

Pushing everything to the back of his mind, he focused all his bandwidth on one task—getting Alex. Opening his eyes, Jake looked through the windshield to see the school was overflowing with cars.

"I guess everyone's here doing the same thing. Pull up there," Jake said, leaning forward and pointing to the closest place to the front entrance where there was space. "I'll be right back."

Opening the door and jumping down from the truck, Mavid hung out the window and yelled, "We'll be here."

Jake walked by groupings of kids and parents, noticing a few of them crying.

"Go home. Stay inside," he said in passing, not looking back. Walking past the front office, he headed down the east corridor, moving directly toward Alex's classroom. Standing outside his son's classroom, Jake saw a boy about to swing an ax, and his wife standing close by. The ax didn't have enough force behind it to sink into the wood and bounced off the door.

"Here, let me do it," Jake said, stepping beside Marie. He didn't need to know what was going on, just that they were all there for the same purpose.

His wife turned and looked stunned to see him there. "Ja...?"

Holding out a hand, he waited for the kid to hand him the ax. "Spike, right?"

Spike handed over the ax and nodded.

"Step back, Spike."

Jake gripped the handle with both hands—quickly looking back to ensure they were in the clear—before heaving the ax over his head and swinging it at the door handle. The head connected, knocking the handle onto the floor. Bracing, he planted a foot into the door, forcing it open.

Screams of shock and surprise sounded from within the classroom. Marie rushed past him into the room and he followed.

"Alex!" she cried, running for their son. "Let him go."

Jake took a quick survey and saw a sea of frightened faces looking at him, including Mrs. Nelson, who was standing at the back of the room clutching onto a student.

"Let her go," he said, raising the ax and pointing it at the teacher.

Mrs. Nelson's eyes narrowed at him, her lips pulling tight to become a thin line, boring into Jake. After a few tension filled moments, she finally released her grasp on Rachel, who fled to where Jake stood. Marie had retrieved Alex and was escorting him out of the classroom.

"Everyone else, out," Jake said to the kids, motioning with his head.

The commotion of motion filled the room as the students wasted no time in rushing for the door. Mrs. Nelson stood planted to the spot by the open window, seething with contempt. When she saw her two helpers also exiting the room, her hands repeatedly clinched and loosened.

When it was just Jake and her, he started to back out of the classroom slowly.

"You can run at your own cost, but the Lord's swift hand of salvation will come for you. All of you. Sinners will die, and I will be there to watch you fall!" Mrs. Nelson shouted, now visibly shaking.

Just before leaving, Jake lowered the ax and said, "Fuck. You," closing the door behind him.

In the time it took him to liberate Alex's classmates, the school had erupted into chaos. Both kids and adults were moving frantically through the corridor as Jake met back up with Marie, Alex, Spike, and the girl Mrs. Nelson had nearly sent to her death.

"Come on. I have a ride for us out front," Jake informed them, grabbing Alex's hand, leading the way.

Forming a human daisy chain, the Wards—along with Rachel and Spike—waded through the stream of people. The line that had been at the front office when he arrived was now gone, leaving a clear shot to the school's entrance. Outside, the five of them paused on the sidewalk, seeing what had set off the chaotic behavior inside.

Bodies of the living dead were roaming around the school's parking lot. Some gave chase to those who weren't in the know, while others screamed as they were caught and being consumed by corpses.

Jake searched for the blue F-150 but didn't see it.

"Damnit! Where the fuck did they go?"

Alex looked up at his dad, wide-eyed from hearing those types of words being used.

"Who?" Marie asked.

"I came here with a couple of friends from the bar. It was a big blue truck."

"Don should be around here somewhere. He... well, he saved my life," Marie replied.

"Don? Shelor?!" Jake exclaimed. "What did that prick do?"

Marie was about to answer when a scream close by cut her off before she could begin.

"Now's not the time. We need to go!"

Knowing she was right, Jake heard the rev of an engine and looked to see Lilly pulling up to the school.

"Get your asses in here," she yelled from the driver's seat.

"That's our ride."

"Woah," Alex said in awe as Jake pulled him along.

Mavid threw open the door for them as they ran for the truck. Marie helped Rachel to get in and was climbing in herself when Alex yelled, "Dad, watch out!"

Jake turned just in time to push his son out of the way and lift the ax he was still carrying, arching it through the air, sinking it into the skull of one of the corpses that had been terrorizing the school. The ax's blade split its head perfectly down the center, cleaving it in two, driving all the way down into its chest.

"Holy shit," Alex and Spike said in unison from inside of the truck.

"Goddamn," Mavid confirmed.

As the body fell to the ground, Jake had to wrench the ax free from the dead person's sternum. Impressed with his quick reaction, he told Alex to scoot over as he climbed in the truck.

"Marie, Alex, eh..."

"Rachel."

"Rachel, Spike. Meet Lilly and Mavid."

Mavid turned, smiling and waving as Lilly threw the Ford into gear. A high-pitched yip sounded from Rachel's lap.

"Oh, and that's Cici."

"Where are we going?" Lilly asked.

"Anywhere but here," Jake replied without a second thought. "Now," he started, turning to Alex, "what was going on with your teacher?"

Chapter Seven

C losing his left eye, he centered the crosshair on the dull bit of skull peeking out from the loose, rotted skin of June Latham, who'd been one of his school teachers as a kid. She had died of a heart attack before he'd finished high school and had attended her funeral with his mother. Now, as Miss Latham clambered over the wrecked car to get to the feeding frenzy that had been the driver, Shipley slowed his breathing before squeezing the trigger. His former teacher's head blew apart in a shower of bone fragments and dried out brain matter as the percussion of the shot bounced around the buildings along Main Street.

Easing away from the scope, he surveyed for the next person.

The sheriff had packed up the rest of the police department's arsenal—which luckily had a hunting rifle and a few dozen rounds—and hauled everything to the rooftop. Taking up a position in a makeshift sniper's nest, he'd been picking off shuffling corpses for the better part of an hour. He'd thinned the herd below to the point he felt confident enough to go out on foot, but decided to stay perched on the rooftop until his supply of ammo ran dry.

He wasted a handful of rounds learning the most viable killing point, which turned out to be a headshot. Police training had taught Shipley to aim for center-mass whenever firing for the greatest chance of success, but when he shot straight through Greg Noble's heart—true to his character when living—the mean, old son of a bitch kept on plodding along.

Shipley's second attempt was to Noble's gut that went seemingly unnoticed. As he cleared the spent shell and cycled another into the breach, the sheriff aimed higher for his third attempt, sending the .30-06 slug through Greg's ear and obliterating the rest of the old man's head as it exited. Noble's body fell to the ground without protest.

Putting his newfound discovery to the test, the sheriff easily picked off two more undead before he had to reload the rifle.

"Just like in the movies," he marveled.

Now, as June Latham laid in the street that was scattered with the dead dead, Shipley took stock of the rifle ammo he had left. Counting out eight loose rounds, he climbed to his feet from the prone position he'd been lying in and stretched, cracking his neck as he did so.

Main Street looked a lot less busy than it had an hour ago, save for a few he couldn't bring himself to put down from having close, personal feelings about—including Barb. A few handguns sat in a duffle bag close by. Though he knew they'd be loaded, the sheriff checked them and then put them back in the bag.

Ready to go back down to street level, Shipley was about to pick up the duffle when he heard the rev of an engine screaming down the road. Looking, he saw a lifted, blue Ford barreling toward the police station, a hoard of dead folks clinging to its sides, and running behind in the truck's wake.

"Goddamnit," he exclaimed and dropped the bag, shouldering the rifle.

As the brakes locked up, the F-150 skidded to a halt, narrowly missing his cruiser still sitting in the middle of the street.

Much more lively zombies pounded and beat on the truck from its bed, the sound of bone scraping against metal piercing the sheriff's ears all the way up on the rooftop.

Looking through the scope, the windows were too tinted to see inside, but Shipley would recognize Jim Adkins' truck anywhere. The driver of the truck reversed and backed up onto the car that had wrecked across the street earlier in the day, bottoming out when the tire went over the trunk, catching the truck's frame. Shipley looked on as the only two tires remaining on the ground spun up plumes of smoke as the driver gunned the gas pedal.

The trail of zombies was catching up to the truck now, swarming over it like ants at a picnic. Taking aim, it was hard to choose which one would make the most difference. Picking the back of a skull—matted and broken hair, grimy with dirt and maggots—Shipley squeezed the trigger.

The bullet tore through the corpse's head as if it were paper, passing into the next corpse, and then the next one. Only the headshot was effective, while the other two came away as if nothing happened.

Kneeling to one knee as he cycled in a new round, he zeroed in on his next target. The remaining ammo went quickly, and by the time it was used, the sheriff didn't know how much good he'd accomplished as more undead came in from all directions. Most looked robbed of their essence from being grave-bound for so long, but a few were freshly dead, people he'd spoken to during the previous few months, or even years.

Shipley threw down the rifle and pulled his sidearm but hesitated, knowing at this range he'd be lucky to hit any viable target. Thinking of his next move, the sheriff grabbed the duffle and headed downstairs.

As he barreled through the door into the station, he hurried to the entrance where the immediate way was clear. Backtracking, he stretched over Barb's desk and grabbed a set of keys she kept stored in a seldom used candy dish. Heading back for the door, Shipley saw the swelling mob preoccupied with the truck that was still attempting to flee.

Turning the handle and throwing the door wide open, he hurried to the side of the station where another, older police cruiser parking lot was. Drawing up to an ancient Ford LTD, he worked the key into the door, unlocking it, before tossing the duffle bag into the passenger seat and sliding in behind the steering wheel.

Lordsland was a small town in rural West Virginia, and the town's budget for law enforcement was razor-thin, and stretched even thinner by penny-pinching bureaucrats like Hamm, or Shumway. It wasn't until a few years ago—when Shipley took the role of Sheriff—he urged the mayor to finally release some funds for new patrol vehicles. Up until that point, "Ramblin' Rose," as the locals liked to call the aged car, was all the town had.

Shipley was good about keeping it maintained, in case one of their newer vehicles went down for repairs, so as he slotted the key into the ignition, he still said a silent prayer before turning it. Grumbling to life, Rose coughed and belched before smoothing out to a low purr.

"Atta girl," he said, shifting the car into reverse and backing out of the spot.

Facing the truck, the sheriff flipped the switches that activated the overhead lights and siren, and pressed the accelerator. The Ford didn't have the giddy up and go like his current patrol car, but she was built like a tank.

Rolling straight for the thickest part of the crowd attacking the truck, Shipley aimed the old car at the back end, hoping to dislodge it from the wrecked vehicle. Tightening his hands on the steering wheel, he braced himself for impact.

Decayed bodies blew apart as the Ford drove through the hoard, while the more fresh dead ones rolled up and over the cruiser, or underneath, causing it to bounce over human speed bumps.

Shipley's eyes shot down just before impact, seeing he was traveling at fifteen miles per hour. He caught the F-150 just behind the rear tire—exactly where he wanted—and shifted the truck enough, in an ad hoc pit maneuver, that the tires were able to grip the road better and began climbing over the car.

Any undead unfortunate enough to be standing close to the right side of the truck disappeared as they were mulched by spinning tires and sprayed all over Shipley's vehicle in a putrid shower of fetid gore.

Pulling hard to the left, he used the car's remaining momentum and stomped the accelerator while switching on the wipers to clear the windshield. Ramblin' Rose crawled through the crowd, bogging down from the sheer number of dead in the street, but Shipley held onto his faith in her and was rewarded with a clearer path ahead.

Somewhere behind him, tires barked as the truck took off down Main Street. Easing the Ford into a U-turn, Shipley followed behind as fast as he could.

Don watched from the driver's seat of his car as chaos broke out all around the school. People seemed to be descending on the place in droves, but he couldn't for the life of him figure out why. He was now regretting being roped into being Marie Ward's undesignated chauffeur.

After the incident with their lawn care guy, his heart had softened a bit toward his otherwise pesky neighbor, but his patience would only go so far, and were wearing thin.

Sitting in the parking lot, he made up his mind. When she came out with her son, he was going to put his foot down, informing Marie he would only be taking her home from the school—no other stops along the way.

Now, as scared looking adults and children ran from scarier looking adults and children, Don's brief moment of chivalry was over. He started his car and waited for the way to clear so he could back out of the parking lot and leave this madness behind.

When a woman and child ran and hid behind another car, he made his move. Shifting into reverse, he whipped the car out with precision, seamlessly shifting into drive, and made for the exit. A large blue pickup truck cut him off before he could drive onto the road that led off school grounds.

"Dickhead!" he yelled, tapping the horn twice.

As he was about to follow, something slammed into the back of his car, causing him to jerk his head around and look. A vagrant looking person was standing near the trunk. Don shifted into park, released his seatbelt, and threw open the driver's door.

"What the shit was that?" he asked, walking toward the rear of the car. "If there's any damage, you'll have to pay for it. This town is going to shit. I swear, I have never in my life seen such craz..." His word hung in the air as he saw the person that ran into his car was missing an arm and part of their lower jaw.

Rheumy eyes, sunken with blackened veins, looked at him. Feeling the hair on his arms stand up, Don slowly stepped back toward the open door. The person's gaze remained locked on him and they started to follow him around the car.

"J-just stay back, buddy. I... It's fine. No harm. Go on about your business."

Don jumped and yelped when he backed into the door, quickly sliding into the driver's seat, pulling the door shut behind him. The person came around and stared at him through the window, pressing their filthy, bloody hand on the glass, smearing it. Don groaned in disgust, facing forward just in time to see Marie, her son, another boy and girl, along with her husband, Jake, jump into the obnoxious truck and screech away.

"That pesky, fucking bitch!" he exclaimed.

Putting the car in drive, Don started to follow, but had to slam on the brakes when a large group of people came running out of the school, failing to look for any oncoming traffic, and disperse across the school grounds.

He looked and saw many of the ones that were already in the parking lot—as well as the people that had come out of the woods—started to chase them.

"Everyone has lost their goddamn minds..." Don said under his breath, shaking his head.

A sudden whoosh from the passenger side of the car caused him to look and see a woman climbing into the seat.

"I'm sorry, but you're going to have get ou—"

Don stopped when the woman pulled out an obscenely large pair of scissors and held them to his throat, the razor-sharp tips digging into his skin.

"Follow that fucking truck," Mrs. Nelson said.

Don swallowed hard, causing the scissors to pierce his skin, sending a weeping trail of blood down his neck. Keeping his movements to a minimum, he eased the car forward, taking extra care while going over the speed bumps.

Leaving the school zone, Don quickly shifted his eyes from the road, catching the briefest of glimpses of the crazed woman holding him hostage, before beginning his pursuit of the truck.

After leaving the school behind, Jake told Lilly to head toward the east side of town, and hopefully out of the infestation of dead that had descended on Lordsland. Rachel was still visibly shaken as Alex and Spike recounted the story of everything that transpired in Mrs. Nelson's classroom.

"Oh my god," Marie said, covering her mouth with one hand as she embraced Rachel with the other.

Mavid turned and faced the backseat. "That's fucked. I knowed that crazy bitch was... well, crazy."

Jake was in shock after hearing about the boy Alex's teacher sent to his death under the guise of religious zealotry. Another reason why he didn't subscribe to the type of organization that could possibly house a following capable of such atrocities—no matter how on the fringe those individuals were.

Lilly had stayed quiet the whole time the kids were giving a play-by-play, but Jake could see her shoulders tense more and more the longer they went on.

"What's the plan, you guys?" she finally asked.

"Get the fuck outta Dodge. Duh," Mavid reiterated.

"No shit, dickhead. But where to? This is fucking crazy and I don't exactly know the protocol when it comes to end of the world events like this."

"Language!" Marie scolded.

Lilly's eyes met hers through the rearview mirror before returning to the road.

"Let's just get out of town first. See what the situation is over in Willow Hill. If it's bad there, too, we keep going until we find a place that isn't completely fu... completely wrecked. Hopefully the military is aware and are sending in—"

Jake stopped when he heard a gunshot ring out as they sped down Main Street. Another shot rang out, causing the kids in the truck to flinch.

"What the hell was that?" Marie asked, forgetting her own rule about cursing.

Everyone in the truck searched for where the shots were coming from. They weren't very loud, but they were close enough for everyone to be concerned whether or not they were being targeted.

"There!" Alex said, pointed up at a rooftop.

Everyone's heads turned to where he was pointing to see the town's sheriff on the rooftop of the police station up ahead. Lilly had slowed to a crawl while searching for the shooter. That had given the undead residents of Lordsland enough time to approach the truck and climb on, beating against any part they could with their grotesque limbs.

"Shit, we're getting swarmed!" Mavid yelled. "Punch it!"

Hitting the gas, everyone in the truck was pressed back in their seats from the sudden acceleration. Weaving down Main Street, Lilly attempted to shake them off with quick jerks.

"Watch out!" Jake screamed.

Gasping, she slammed the brakes to keep from hitting a wrecked car across from the police station. The truck was rolling with too much momentum and went up and over the back end of the car. Everyone inside the truck was tossed and bounced around the cab, Cici squawking as Rachel clutched the little dog to her chest.

"Is everyone okay?" Jake asked, holding the right side of his head where it had smacked off the window.

With affirmations they were, everyone settled back into their seats, though slanted now.

"Christ, woman. I thought I was goner on that one," Mavid said.

"Zip it," Lilly said, looking worried.

"What is it?" Marie asked.

"I think we're stuck," Jake offered.

"No, we're not," Lilly corrected.

"Dad, look," Alex said.

Jake looked out the same window his head had ricocheted off moments before, only to see Sheriff Shipley standing on the rooftop across the street. He wanted to roll the window down and communicate with the man, but knew the dead people that were assaulting the truck would try to get in. Plus the roar of the engine, along with spinning tires, made it hard to hear much of anything.

"Give it a rest. You're gonna blow it u—"

Mavid was cut off by the crack of a gunshot from close by. Jake's head whipped around to see to the head of a young lady with spikes of metal protruding from her mouth explode, sending a wave of soupy brains splattering across the window. He looked up just as the sheriff was taking aim again. Another shot rang out. And then another.

"Even though the son of a bitch has thrown me in the drunk tank more than I care to admit, he sure is a damn good shot," Mavid admitted, slapping his knee as they watched another corpse drop to the ground.

"Fucking language!" Marie chided, causing the three kids to giggle.

Jake kept count in his head while watching Shipley take out a total of eight rotting people.

"Lilly!" Mavid yelled.

"I'm rocking it. Shut it!" she replied.

Jake turned and faced Marie and the kids. Alex and Spike were looking around at everything happening outside of the truck, a wild excitement in their eyes. Rachel had her head down, petting Cici to keep them both calm. Marie met his eyes, fear hiding behind the brave front she was putting on. He wanted nothing more than to reach out and grab her hands, to pull her in close and whisper in her ear that everything was going to be alright, but the wound from this morning was still fresh.

Just as he was about to offer her an olive branch, sirens started to wail from the police station. Jake turned to look just in time and warned everyone to brace for impact.

"Hold on!"

Grabbing Marie and Alex, Jake tried to huddle against them—as well as Rachel and Spike—when the police car slammed into the truck.

"Get off of me, old man," Lilly said, pushing Mavid back over to the passenger seat.

She'd miraculously kept her foot on the gas pedal and the truck started to climb higher over the car. "Come on, you bitch!"

Tires continued to spin, but the truck had shifted enough to gain a bit of traction.

"Oh my god," Marie said, her face ashen as she looked past Jake out the window.

A spray of shredded human bits was rooster-tailing over the truck.

"That is so gross," Rachel said, disgusted.

"Wicked," Spike added.

Jake leaned on the window, seeing the dead that had been attacking the right side of the truck were now being chewed up by the spinning tires. His stomach churned as the smell of death intensified from the display of macabre aromatics that permeated the truck's interior.

The rocking cab of the Ford fell off the car, hitting the road hard, but was able to keep rolling, mowing over stumbling dead that were unfortunate enough to be standing in its path.

Barking the tires as they sped down Main Street, Jake looked back and saw the sheriff was in hot pursuit of them.

Don was doing his best to keep up with the big blue Ford. It wasn't easy with the sharp scissors stabbing into his neck, but he thought he was doing a more than outstanding job—considering the circumstances.

The crazed woman sat in the seat beside him, a permanent smile scrolled across her face, while she hummed a tune low, rocking back and forth.

A shot rang out, causing them both to jump. The scissors drew another line of blood on Don's neck.

"Ease up there, cowboy. Looks like they're slowing down. I don't want them to know we're back here," Mrs. Nelson explained.

Don did as he was told. "My name is Donald Shelor. Not 'cowboy.' I would appreciate it if you at least addressed me by my name if you're going to hold me hostage." Don's voice was stern, yet fear lingered in its undertone.

"Okay, Donald Shelor. We need to stay at a reasonable distance from the sinners until I'm shown the path before us."

Don stopped his car in the middle of the street and looked around. "If we stay here—stationary—these... things will overrun us."

"Put your faith in the Lord, Donald Shelor. He will protect us from the scourge that walks the earth now."

Waiting for the creatures to start attacking the car at any moment, he sat, mystified, as they continued on, ignoring them while in pursuit of the Ford.

"Look! They've been detained by His almighty power."

Farther down Main Street, the blue truck appeared to have wrecked, and was stuck on top of another car. Gunshots reverberated from somewhere up ahead.

"Can you see who is shooting? I don't see anyone," Don asked.

"It does not matter. Nothing in this world does," Mrs. Nelson replied.

Don's lips tightened into a flat line. He was catching onto the woman's schtick, and it was starting to grate on him.

"Listen, I don't know what this is all about, but I think you're going about this the wron—"

Suddenly, the backdoor to the car opened, and a woman climbed inside.

"Shit, man. I didn't think anyone was ever going to stop," the stranger said.

Both Don and Mrs. Nelson turned to see a woman—barely wearing anything at all—sitting in the backseat.

"Hey, are y'all some kinda freaks or something? I've done couples before, but the scissors... fuck it, I'm down. Fifty now, fifty when we're done."

Don saw the crazy woman's brow furrow deeply and then relax with clarity. "Christina? Christina Schommer?" Mrs. Nelson asked.

The stranger's eyes narrowed in on the woman in the front seat. Don could actually see the cogs in her mind turning, trying to place where she knew the woman from.

"Mrs. Nelson? Holy shit, is that really you? I thought you'd have died by now. Tight-assed bitch. Too fuckin' mean, I guess."

Mrs. Nelson bared her teeth at the girl. "You always did have a filthy mouth, even as a young girl. And I see you've done absolutely nothing with your life. Stray as far from the path as one could."

"Shiiiit. I've done plenty. Fucked my way from one side of this town to the other, and back again. Even went to Vegas a few times. What about you, Dreama? You let anyone blow the dust outta that bear trap of yours? Or are you still in mourning for your husband that died, what, before I was even born?"

"I will not be spoken to like this!" Mrs. Nelson yelled, grinding the scissors into Don's neck, causing him to spudder. "You take that mouth, and sinful ways, out of this car. Right now!"

Christina threw up a middle finger in Mrs. Nelson's face. "Me and my mouth ain't going nowhere. I bet this guy won't argue," she added, winking at Don. "I'd even let you have a ride on it, if you're payin'."

Don shuddered at the thought of soliciting the hooker. In the brief time he'd known the woman in his backseat, it was clear to him why she hadn't been attacked by one of the creatures outside—she looked like she was one of them, only slightly less dead than the ones wandering the streets.

"Hey, uh, Dreama?" Don said, looking ahead.

Mrs. Nelson looked around and saw a police car had now joined the fray. It appeared as though it had run into the truck, setting it free, and was swinging into a U-turn to follow it.

"Go after them," Mrs. Nelson said, twisting the scissors.

Without a word, Don pressed the gas, following the cop car.

"This is without a doubt the third craziest date I've been on," Christina said from the back. "Just behind the time a guy asked me to stick a deflated balloon in his ass and blow it up until it popped. And that one time a date took me to Applebee's."

Don and Mrs. Nelson's eyes met for a moment, both too intrigued for their own good.

"What happened at Applebee's?" Don asked.

Chapter Eight

The big Ford was driving rougher now after the impact by the police cruiser. Lilly was doing her best to handle it, constantly correcting it to keep the truck on the road.

"This thing is fucked. Shipley may have gotten us out of that jam, but he knocked something loose in the back," Lilly said before grunting as she worked the steering wheel.

"We're not far from route twenty. That'll take us to Willow Hill. Will it last that long?" Jake asked.

"Maybe. I'll damn sure try to get us outta here."

While Lilly was trying to limp the truck along to greener pastures, Jake checked on everyone in the back.

"Hey, sweetie, are you doing alright?" he asked Rachel.

She looked up at him and nodded, Cici wagging her tail in the girl's lap to signal she, too, was okay. Jake shifted his eyes to Spike, who gave an enthusiastic thumb's up and continued watching the dead people outside pan by. Jake's gaze finally settled on Alex and Marie, both looking wary from the chaos that had befallen their town.

"How are you two doing?" he asked.

Even though Alex had proclaimed himself a man now—last year during a pool party—and his friends were in spitting distance, he reached out for Jake to comfort him. Jake pulled his son onto his lap and rocked him. To their left, Marie's body shook in silent sobs as she watched her husband and son together, catching Jake's eye. He looked at her, still furious with her betrayal, yet still reached out and took her hand in his, seeing her wince as he did and looked down to her hands wrapped in bandages for the first time.

"Holy fuck," Mavid said from the front.

Jake shifted Alex over so he could see what was going on. A few hundred yards up ahead was a literal wall of undead headed straight for them.

"What do I do?" Lilly asked.

"Uhhh..." Jake's mind went blank.

"Here. Turn here. Now!" Mavid said, pointing to a road going off to the right.

Lilly cut the wheel sharp, sending the passengers of the truck to the left side of the cab—Spike yelling about being crushed—until the truck straightened out and they were gliding along the asphalt again.

Jake looked behind and saw Sheriff Shipley make the turn, continuing to follow along behind them.

"Where the hell are you taking me, old man?" Lilly asked.

"Just keep going straight 'til we get to the Oakvale intersection, then hang another right," Mavid replied.

"Right at Oakvale inter... are you taking us out Hi-Ho Way?" Lilly grumbled, turning to scowl at Mavid.

"Indeed, I am. Who better to align ourselves with than someone that's ready for the end of the world? Hmmmmmmm?" Mavid said matter of factly.

"What's Hi-Ho Way? Who lives out there?" Marie asked, voicing the questions everyone in the back had on their minds.

Lilly scoffed, leaving it up to Mavid to fill them in on the details.

"I got a buddy that lives out there. Only him and his animals. NO NEIGHBORS. He's kinda the... eccentric type. Doomsday prepper.

Has been living off grid for over two decades, if I remember correctly. Completely self-sufficient."

"Okay," Jake said, "but what's Lilly's problem with this guy?"

Jake looked up and saw their driver staring daggers at him in the rearview mirror. He swallowed hard before saying, "But it's really none of our business. Not really."

"L.T. and our pretty little Lilly here were a thang at one time or another. Didn't end well. And that's putting it lightly," Mavid explained.

"Pfft," sounded from their driver.

"Lilly swore off men after they split, and L.T. came away with one ear less than when they started dating. I had the absolute pleasure of mediating the assets between them because they refused to speak to one another," Mavid continued.

"You cut off some dude's ear?" Jake asked.

The daggers turned into a thousand needles in the mirror as her eyes formed slits, all aimed directly at Jake.

"What assets?" Marie asked.

A low croak issued from Mavid's throat as he looked over at Lilly.

"Fuckin' tell 'em. They know most of it now, anyway," she said.

"Well, there was a cat, two dogs, and a whole mess of goats. Animals, mostly."

"*Mostly.*"

"Mmm," Mavid started. "And McGoo's."

"The bar?" Jake said.

"The bar," Mavid confirmed.

"Oof."

"Big fuckin' oof," Lilly said.

"Language, please," Marie reminded, looking around at the kids.

"Well, obviously Lilly got the bar," Jake pointed out.

"L.T. got all the goats and the dogs," Mavid continued on, "Lilly got the bar and the cat."

"And that fucker's ear," she said with a wide grin.

"And that fucker's ear," Mavid confirmed.

"Language," Jake said this time.

Feeling the truck slow, Jake looked and saw a handmade sign at the intersection they were approaching that read "Hi-Ho Way." Lilly aggressively hit the turn signal to let Shipley know which direction they were going. Pulling off the pavement, the truck rumbled onto a dirt road that was being overgrown by brush.

The first thought that occurred to him as they traveled along the road was how few dead people there were. In fact, Jake took a moment—looking out every window and seeing none—before saying, "Huh."

"What?" Marie asked.

"There aren't any of those things out here," he replied.

Everyone else in the cab looked out into the surrounding woods, confirming Jake's observation.

"Has to be L.T.'s doing. He don't play around when it comes to trespassers. I once saw him take down a wild boar with a spork during rutting season cause it was trying to break down his fence to get to his sows," Mavid told them. "Damndest thing I'd ever seen't."

All three kids sat in awe, Spike being the only one to say anything. "Woah."

Jake saw Lilly's fingers tighten on the steering wheel before relaxing. "We'll be there in a minute," she announced.

A moderately sized compound of buildings and pens came into view through the windshield. A large, decommissioned military truck sat off to the left, and an International Scout sat to the right of it.

"No one try to get out until we're given the signal," Lilly told them as she stopped the truck in a small clearing. She started tapping on the horn, beeping it in a strange pattern.

Jake looked around and saw that the same, confused look on his face was mimicked on everyone else's in the backseat. He started to ask what was happening, but Mavid held up his shaking hand, cutting him off just as he was starting. Hearing the crunch of gravel, he turned and saw the sheriff pulling up behind them. Shipley seemed to know whatever the protocol was when coming onto L.T.'s property, sitting behind the wheel while looking around, his eyes occasionally wandering up to the trees.

Feeling antsy, he wanted answers as to what was going on when something dropped down in front of the truck. Pure instinct made him reach for the ax laying on the floorboard.

Slowly rising before them, a lump of leaves raised its arms and uncovered its head. The man beneath was smiling ear to scar.

"And that's why I'm not allowed at Applebee's anymore. Any of them," Christina said.

Don's stomach clenched as he felt bile rising in his throat. He'd never heard such depravities in his life and wanted nothing more than a hot shower. The scissor wielding woman to his right was dry heaving into her lap, repeatedly moving her free hand from her head to her sternum, and then from shoulder to shoulder.

"For fuck's sake, y'all need to get out more. Ain't nothing wrong with a swizzlin' now and then," Christina said from the backseat. "You know... if you two wanted me to show you a thing or two, it'd be on the house. Just this one time."

Don and Mrs. Nelson both shouted no in unison, their eyes lingering on one another for a moment.

"Fine," Christina pouted. "Where are we going, anyway?"

Mrs. Nelson turned her head slightly to address the question. "We're on a mission from God."

"Uh huh. Okay. Cool. Can we go to Donna's and get some food? I got a hankerin' for some eggs and bacon," Christina said.

"No!" Mrs. Nelson aimed the scissors at her, then quickly jabbed them back to Don's neck.

"T-they're turning it looks like," Don said.

Christina leaned forward in between the front seats and stared. "Is that who we're chasing? That's a fuckin' cop!"

"Sit back!" Mrs. Nelson chastised. "You, keep your distance and pay attention. Follow them wherever they go."

"Calm your tits, Dreama. Sheesh."

Mrs. Nelson squeezed her eyes shut, rolling her head while rotating her shoulders. When Don went to make the turn, he side-glanced over and saw the building tension was visible on her face. Though he didn't approve of the woman's lifestyle that was currently occupying the backseat, she may just be the godsend he needed to get out of this insane situation he found himself in.

"Ugh, all these weeds are going to scratch up the paint," he complained.

"There are bigger issues at hand. Sinners must be dealt with in the appropriate manner. Starting with the lot we're following."

"You still talk like an asshole, too," Christina commented. "I'm sooooo hungrhee-hee-hee," she continued, screeching the last word while mimicking a stabbing motion into her stomach.

"Easy for you to say, it's not your car," Don grumbled under his breath.

"You two will be silent! I will not listen to your pathetic complaining, or whoring ways, any longer. Is that clear?" Mrs. Nelson asked, raking the sharp tips of the scissors over the skin of Don's neck.

"Yeah, sure. Shit," Christina replied.

Don clenched his jaw, threatening to crack his teeth from the force. "As crystal," he said.

The harried school marm blew out a breath of frustration. Loose strands of hair had fallen from the tight bun on top of her head, wisping around her face in an ethereal quality.

"Dreama?" Christina asked.

Mrs. Nelson turned her stoic face toward the woman and raised her eyebrows.

"Exactly how many people are we chasing currently?"

Thinking for a moment, she said, "At least half a dozen. Why?"

Christina nodded. "Oh."

"Why?!"

Christina's eyes went wide as she looked out the window. "So, you're chasing down half a dozen 'sinners' and all you have is a pair of scissors? I don't know, seems kinda... crazy to me."

Before Mrs. Nelson could reply, Don pulled the car to a stop in the middle of the dirt road.

"Why are we not following them?" Mrs. Nelson asked.

Don nodded his head forward, instantly regretting it as the scissors dug deeper into the meat of his neck. "They've stopped. Just up ahead. I can't see what's going on from here."

Leaning forward between the front seats again, realization washed over Christina's face. "Fuck me, this is L.T.'s Place."

Shipley saw a blur drop and disappear in front of the Ford truck. He'd been searching for L.T. since pulling onto the man's property, knowing the recluse was well aware of their impending arrival long before they parked.

Drawing his sidearm as he climbed out of Ramblin' Rose, he slowly skirted around the truck—along the driver's side—and made his way toward the front.

L.T. popped up, unshrouding his head from the hood he was wearing and smiled.

"Afternoon, Sheriff. To what do I owe the pleasure of your presence on my land?" L.T. asked.

Shipley's eyes narrowed and they searched the surrounding area. "Don't know if you're aware of what's been going on around town, but we have a bit of a situation."

L.T.'s face relaxed a bit, shifting into a smirk. "You talking about all them dead folks walking around, are ya? Shit, I thought that was normal. We're all dead, Sheriff. We just don't know it until it's too late."

Shipley wanted to chuckle at the man's backwoods, philosophical observations, but he remained true to his discipline, keeping his face void of emotions. "Am I good to lower this thing, or is it still necessary?" he asked, slightly raising the gun in his hands.

Standing up straighter, L.T. brought up his hands that were holding a shotgun and hooked it to a clip on his belt. "Certainly, Sheriff. Mi casa, es su casa," the man said.

Shipley lightened his grip on the sidearm and re-holstered it. The passenger door of the truck swung open and Mavid's head came popping out.

"What are you doing, you old fucking buzzard?"

He and L.T. started laughing as Mavid made his way around the truck, culminating in an embrace shared by the two men.

"How the hell did they drag you away from your barstool? I didn't even think nukes dropping could accomplish such a feat," L.T. remarked.

Mavid gave a hearty laugh. "Someone had to make sure these people weren't killed by all those rotten fuckers."

L.T.'s face took on a grim facade. "Yeah, I got a pile of 'em out back. Was planning to burn 'em after dark. Big Fred paid me a visit early this morning, so I knew some kinda shit had hit the fan."

"Big Fred, huh?" Mavid pondered. "Never did like that prick. Glad he's dead... again."

Everyone started to file out of the truck, Lilly being the last.

The second Rachel's feet touched the ground, Cici began squirming in her arms, eventually working free and hit the ground running.

"Hey, come back! It's not safe out there," the girl yelled, a frown spreading over her mouth.

"Well, shit-fire. Look what the cat dragged in," L.T. quipped with a wide grin. "Knowed you was too mean to let a little ol apocalypse get you down."

Shipley saw the woman make a face and raise her middle finger at the man, a salute to his loose tongue.

"You done brought the whole kit 'n kaboodle, didn't ya, darlin'?"

Shipley stepped between the former lovers, raising his hands. "For the sake of the children's eyes and, uh, ears, let's keep it friendly. Okay?"

Lilly rolled her eyes while L.T. continued to grin, keeping his eyes locked on her. Jake stepped forward and introduced himself to the prepper then went down the line with everyone else's names.

"Pleased to meet y'all. Now, why are y'all here exactly?" L.T. asked, eyeing the sheriff.

Shipley looked around at the other. "I don't know, I just followed them here."

Lilly continued to look away while Jake and Marie's gazes fell on Mavid.

"Well, we were gettin' the fuck outta Dodge, but hit a snag when we tried to leave. Way more of them damn thangs than we thought possible. Had to think quick and your little slice of Heaven here was the closest oasis from all the fuckery," Mavid explained.

L.T. nodded slowly. "I see, I see. Now, as some of you well know," his eyes shifting between Mavid, Lilly, and Shipley, "I'd normally tell you to fu— to get lost." L.T. looked at Rachel, Alex, and Spike guiltily after correcting himself. "But since this is a once in a lifetime..." he searched for the right word, "event, I'm feelin' a little more generous with what's mine. As I told the sheriff here, mi casa, es su casa."

Mavid clapped L.T. on his shoulder, turning to face the others with a genuine smile on his face. "Good to hear, cause I could really use a drink, if you know what I mean," he said, winking.

"I gotcha, old timer. But I do have one question for all of you," L.T. said.

"What's that?" Mavid asked.

"Who is that following y'all in the other car?"

Everyone's head turned in unison to look down the dirt road.

Don eyed the scissors as his crazed captor waved them around in his face, emphasizing her words by jabbing them toward his eyes.

"This is our final stand. The moment when we vanquish evil and send these heathens back to the depths of Hell. We will be welcomed with open arms into His loving embrace. We are His agents. We must not fail Him." Mrs. Nelson was breathing hard, chest heaving, and her face flushing red.

"I hear you. But we can't... I don't understand what we're supposed to do about it," Don said, meekly.

Mrs. Nelson glowered at him.

"Neither does she," Christina butted in. "She's just regurgitating the same nonsense she has been saying for years. Dreama's mind is twisted from too much self-imposed isolation from the actual world we live in that she can't see her own hypocrisy." She stretched and yawned before continuing on. "If she really cared about helping people, saving them from themselves, she would've been out there volunteering her time and energy. No, she sits around in judgment. Puh-theh-tic."

The movement was quicker than Don could track, but he threw up his hand to cover his face when his reactionary sensors blared in his head. A feral growl filled the car, then a scream. Peeking through his fingers, Don saw the woman had lunged into the backseat. Peering over the headrest, he saw a mixture of shock and anger coming off Christina's face in waves.

The school teacher jerked away, settling back into the front passenger seat, the scissors and the hand holding them were covered in blood. Don looked again to see arterial blood blooming across the woman's skimpy clothes. Fear squeezed his heart as his hand fumbled for the door handle.

Finding it, Don pressed himself against the door, spilling out onto the ground while trying to keep an eye on Mrs. Nelson.

"Get back in here!" she shrieked after realizing what was going on.

Don gathered himself enough to make it to his feet, pausing for a moment to take in the sight of the savagery written on the woman's face. His feet slid on the gravel, nearly sending him back to the ground, but he was able to gain traction and took off down the road in the direction they had come.

As he fled, her shouts of threats fell on deaf ears, and he threw up a middle finger as a parting gift.

The group made their way down the dirt road to figure out what L.T. was talking about. The prepper took point, with the others following close behind—Mavid bringing up the rear. As the car came into view, Jake and Marie both spoke at the same time.

"That looks like Don's car," Marie said.

"What the fuck is Don doing out here?" Jake asked.

L.T. paused, causing the group to ripple to a stop. "You know the owner?" he asked.

"Yeah, he's our neighbor. Complete dick," Jake answered.

"Jake..." Marie started.

He turned to her and shrugged. "It's not not true."

She gave him a stern look similar to one Don would and he wanted to laugh, but stifled it.

L.T. broke away from the group, edging down the side of the road, Spike breaking ranks and opting to follow him as they checked the vehicle out.

"Someone's in the back," L.T. told the others. "Wounded. Oh shit, is that..."

As he was about to say a name, a yell rang out from the woods. Everyone jumped back, expecting one of the dead things to attack. L.T. slid over the hood of the car to evade whatever it was, while Spike turned to run, but was grabbed from behind and jerked close to the attacker.

Cold steel pressed into the boy's throat and the others gave out a collective gasp, a panic-stricken screeching issuing from Rachel's mouth.

Mrs. Nelson held her student at scissor-point, glaring at the group.

"Godless savages. I warned you. All of you!" Her head shot to the right. "You, sinner, with the others. Now!" she said to L.T., motioning with her head for him to join the rest of the group standing in the middle of the road.

Jake saw the defiance in the man's eyes, knew he didn't take to being ordered around too kindly. "L.T., over here. Please," Jake requested, practically begging to ensure Spike's safety.

L.T. looked at Jake and then the others, the tension in his shoulders going slack as he begrudgingly joined them.

"How do you not understand by now? Every single one of you is damned. You rot in the flesh you wear and your souls wither from your wicked ways," Mrs. Nelson told them, jerking Spike's head to the side by pulling his hair.

Jake looked deep into her eyes, seeing the deep-seeded confusion; desperation hiding behind a layer of fear that was dressed in a neat, outward appearing, unassuming school teacher. He didn't give a fuck what she was saying, but scared with how far she was prepared to go to get her point across.

"Please," he said, taking a step forward, "let him go. He doesn't understand what you're talking about. He's just a kid."

Mrs. Nelson's eyes went blank for a moment, losing focus. Her face contorted into sinister glee. Reaffirming her grip on Spike's head, she raised the scissors high into the air.

"In His name, the innocent shall remain intact!" she yelled.

Marie cried out, Rachel burying her head into the crook of her arm. L.T., Mavid, and Alex all shouted for the woman to stop. Shipley's hand went to his sidearm, hoping his draw was fast enough. Jake was about to lunge forward, hoping to save the boy, when movement from behind the school teacher caught his eye.

"You're such a fucking cunt, Dreama," Christina said from behind before a shot echoed through the valley.

Spike was released from death's grip, rushing forward to join the others. Jake watched—as if in slow motion—as the school teacher's skull blew apart; a shower of skull fragments and brain matter painted the forest behind the woman as she fell to the ground.

Christina stood, staring at the group, lowering the gun as her arm dangled loosely at her side, slapping against her hip while she wobbled on unsteady legs.

"Who the fuck are all of you?" she asked before crumpling into a heap on top of Mrs. Nelson.

Doc Butler had been inundated with calls since before sunrise from the residents of Lordsland. Being a small town doctor had its perks, sure, but it was days like today that he regretted not retiring sooner.

Curse my big, soft heart, he thought as he sat in his office, the door barred with his oversized desk.

After he'd arrived at his office earlier in the morning, he was greeted by a parking lot full of patients, ranging from the typical, early on-set seasonal flu, to more minor injuries incurred from the storm that swept through the area overnight. Butler kept his best bedside smile on his face as he made his way inside.

He waved at Lizz, his receptionist, before heading to his personal office. Tossing his bag into a vacant chair, he settled in behind his desk and picked up the phone. The doc hadn't heard from his daughter in a few days, and he'd got wind she'd been running around with Jerry, a natural born loser in Butler's eyes.

As the phone rang to call his daughter, he was starting to second guess his decision about having a kid so late in life. He just didn't understand today's youth.

After the tenth ring, he knew it was a lost cause, but made a mental note to call Anna back during his lunch hour. Butler busied himself with the morning paper—specifically the sports section to check on his beloved 49ers—before reading over the first chart of the day.

A knock sounded at the door before Lizz said from the other side, "Arthur, we're getting a lot of people piling into the office."

Butler sighed inwardly. "Thank you," he replied. "I'll be out in a minute."

Standing from his desk, he donned his white overcoat, thinking back, trying to remember the last time such an influx of patients came rushing in.

Bird flu? he pondered. *Or was Y2K,* the folks around town not realizing it was a computer glitch and not something that was communicable.

Looking at himself in the mirror, his already tired eyes told him a single truth: it was going to be a long day. Haggard, he left his office.

By lunch, Butler's internal battery was drained after seeing a record breaking twenty patients in four hours. Most had been simple complaints of aches and pains—to which he recommended a dose or two of Advil before sending them on their way—while two people were expressing more concerning symptoms of severe, flu-like signs. Butler highly recommended they visit the ER over in Willow Hill after finding it hard to get an accurate vitals reading from them.

Feeling as though he was coming up for air after a long dive in the ocean, he peeked into the waiting area to see it was full again—this bunch looked a lot more sickly than the previous patients. Catching the eye of his receptionist, Butler motioned with his head for her to meet him in the back and closed the door.

"What in Sam Hill is going on today?" he asked. "What are they saying is wrong?"

Lizz hesitated with her answer for a moment. "Well, that's kinda the funny thing about it. Most of the ones that are out there never signed in for an appointment. They just wandered in here and sat in the lobby. I tried to talk to a few, ask them what they wanted to be seen for, but they just stared off into space."

Doc Butler stroked his chin for a moment, wondering if some new strain of something was starting to go around. "Lizz, I may have to dip out early today. I haven't been able to get a hold of Anna for a couple of days and I need to make sure she's okay."

He could see Lizz's internal conflict playing out through her eyes.

"And I suppose you want me to inform them all that they'll have to come back another day?" she asked.

Butler grinned. "I knew there was a reason I kept you around," he joked. "I need to grab a few things from my office first. Then I'm gone. Thank you, Lizz."

"Mmhmm," she replied, walking back toward the lobby.

In his office, Butler grabbed his jacket from the coat rack after shedding his white overcoat, swapping them out. Stepping behind his desk, he picked up the phone and tried Anna's apartment again. With no answer, he called home. His wife answered, talking loudly over the dogs barking in the background.

"Hello?"

"Hey, I'm calling it a day at the office. I'm going to go over to Anna's and see if she's there and why she isn't answering."

"Huh? Okay," Dee said.

"What's going on there?" Butler asked.

"I... I don't know. They've been doing this all morning. Just pacing around, staring out the doors and windows. Barking non-stop." The irritation in his wife's voice was overwhelmingly evident.

"I'll be there as soon as I can. An hour, tops," Butler said, hoping to calm his wife's nerves.

"Okay. Be careful. We can figure out din—"

A scream came from somewhere in the doctor's office, causing him to jerk his head away from the receiver.
"What was that?" Dee asked.

He left his wife's question hanging in the air as he strained his ears, trying to listen. Another scream came, cutting off midway through.

Butler let the phone fall to the floor as he left his office, his wife stranded on the other end.

In the hallway between his office and the exam rooms, Butler could hear faint groaning coming from the lobby. Edging up to the door, apprehension building, he turned the handle slowly, pulling it open just enough to see through with one eye.

Chills rippled over his skin at the scene playing out in the lobby. Lizz was laying on the floor, her head lulling from side to side. The patients that had been waiting there were all leaned over the receptionist, blood and gore spreading over the carpet at an alarming rate.

"Dear God..." Butler exclaimed.

By speaking, he inadvertently alerted Lizz's attackers. Turning to face him, the doc saw something impossible—Billy Jenkins, one of Butler's childhood friends that had died a few years prior, was now staring at him through half-sunken, dilapidated eyes.

Butler started to back away as the others continued to eviscerate Lizz. Billy rose to his feet, dried pieces of flesh shaking off his frame as he followed Butler into the hallway.

"Billy... you're dead," he said to his long-deceased friend.

The corpse said nothing as it stalked the doctor all the way to his office. Fumbling for the door handle, Butler was barely able to slip in and close the door as Billy thumped against it on the other side.

When he finally broke out of the shock of what he'd just seen, Butler picked up the phone receiver from the floor, hung it up, before picking up to dial 911. The phone rang for a solid minute before he gave up and replaced the receiver back on the cradle. A million thoughts shot through his head in the space of seconds, none coherent enough to grasp onto and focus his mind on.

Picking up the phone again, he tried to call Dee back, with the result being the same as 911 services. Now he was worried about his wife on top of his missing daughter, and his receptionist was being eaten in the lobby of his medical practice.

The thumping at the door grew louder, and Billy started to moan out a dry rattle. Butler stood frozen for a moment, thinking of his next move. He needed to get out of the office, but the door past the lobby was the closest exit aside from the one that led to the back alleyway.

Billy's attacks on the door grew more aggressive, shaking the doc out of thought. Looking around his office for inspiration, Butler's eyes lingered on one of his wife's needlepoints.

Adapt. Overcome. Achieve.

Dee opted to use crimson and gold threading, a sign she really didn't mind his love of the 49ers despite her constant ribbing. Checking the drawers of his desk, there was little in the way of proper self-defense implements. The best thing he had on-hand was a six-foot coat rack in the corner, and letter opener.

Pulling his doctor's coat from the rack, he slipped it on and put the letter opener in one of its pockets.

Turning away from the door—where Billy was still demanding an audience with the doc—Butler faced the large window behind his desk. Heaving the rack's heavy base up and wielding it like a lance, he charged at the window, putting as much force and momentum behind the thrust as he could.

The base pinged off the thick glass, sending a shockwave up the rack and into Butler's hands, causing him to drop it.

"Duh," he said, bending to pick it up off the floor.

Standing parallel to the window, he cocked the coat rack back like a baseball bat, took a deep breath, and swung, connecting the edge of the base with glass, sending a shower of glass outward onto the grass and leaves.

Raking away loose shards from the frame, Butler tossed the rack outside. Looking back, the picture of him, Anna, and Dee drew his gaze for a moment. He was determined to see them both again.

Looking up at the door, shaking from the pounding, he said, "Later, Billy," before hoisting himself out of the window to the ground below. His old knees buckled as he landed, his right foot catching the coat rack in the process, sending him skidding forward.

"Oh, geez," he said weakly as he rolled over.

Catching his breath, Butler turned and looked toward the side of the building that was closest to Main Street. Wave after wave of undead, shambling folks moved in a steady stream toward downtown Lordsland.

His eyes grew wide and he struggled to regain his feet. Knees popping, he grabbed the coat rack and moved into the forest behind his office, away from the horde.

Chapter Nine

By the time Jake and L.T. were able to get Christina into L.T.'s house and place her on his couch, Jake was sucking deep gulps of air—the alcohol still lingering in his system—gassed from carrying the woman up the long driveway. Both men fell into one of the recliners in the room as the others filed in behind them.

"Woah, this place is rad," Alex said, his eyes darting around the living room, unable to settle on a single thing.

L.T. chuckled hoarsely. "Think so, kid? It's alright, I guess."

Lilly scoffed at the remark, looking as though she'd rather be outside with the walking dead rather than back in the house she once shared with its owner.

Marie rushed past everyone, kneeling at the couch Christina was lying on to access the woman's wounds.

"I need gauze or something. And alcohol," she said to anyone that was listening. No one rushed to get up or offer a hand.

Lilly rolled her eyes. "I think I still remember where that stuff is. Be right back."

Alex, Rachel, and Spike took a seat on a long couch sitting under a wall that held trophy kills mounted on it. Jake saw his son was still dazzled by much manlier decor than he was used to at their home. Mavid took a spot on the hall tree next to the front door, breathing out a heavy sigh.

Shipley lingered at the door for a moment. "I have some stuff in the cruiser that might help. I will be back directly," he said just before leaving.

Finally feeling rested, Jake sat forward in the chair, facing Marie. "How's she doing?" he asked.

His wife looked at Christina, then at him, her face telling him all he needed to know. "She's lost a lot of blood. Still losing it."

L.T. rose to his feet suddenly. "I'll be right back."

Jake watched him walk into a different part of the house, opposite of the way Lilly had gone. Just as he left, Lilly came back holding a handful of towels and a bottle of whiskey.

"Here," she said, holding the bottle out to Marie.

Taking it, Marie quickly twisted off the cap and lifted Christina's shirt, revealing an angry looking hole in the woman's abdomen.

"Hold her down," she said, looking up at Jake.

Bending over the couch, Jake placed his hands on the woman's shoulders, pressing down with his body weight. Marie upended the bottle over the wound, causing Christina to come to life, flailing at the pain from the alcohol.

"Towels," Marie said, holding out her hand.

Lilly gave her two and stepped over to help Jake hold down the bucking woman. Whistling echoed into the room, preceding L.T.'s return. He stepped back into the living room holding a large plastic case in a gloved hand, and a butane torch in the other.

L.T.'s eyes shifted to the bottle sitting on the floor. "Is that my good shit? Dammit, I was saving that for a special occasion!"

"Ain't the end of the world special enough to dip into good stuff?" Mavid asked, also eying the bottle, licking his lips.

L.T. simply shook his head as he placed the case on the coffee table. Pausing as he passed the couch Christina was now squirming around on, he disappeared in the same direction Lilly had come back from with the towels.

Marie held the folded towels over the wound, blood starting to seep through onto her hands. L.T. came back into the living room, posing with a large spoon like it was a torch, and he was lady liberty. Alex, Spike, and Rachel all giggled at the man's antics.

Returning to the coffee table, L.T. picked up the torch, pulling the trigger ignitor until a flame caught, burning a rich shade of blue.

"Woah," Rachel said.

"Might want to give her a drink of that," Mavid suggested, pointing to the whiskey bottle.

Christina had calmed down enough for Jake to manage on his own, so Lilly bent, grabbing the bottle, and brought it up to the wounded woman's lips.

"Drink, darlin'," she told her.

Christina took a large gulp of whiskey, then opened her mouth for another. "That is some good shit," she agreed, smiling.

"Told ya," L.T. said as he held the torch to the spoon, the metal starting to glow red. "Get ready, she ain't gonna like this."

Jake braced himself against Christina's shoulders as Lilly rejoined him.

"I can't watch!" Rachel said, covering her eyes with her hands.

Spike and Alex looked on from the couch in fascination, while Mavid looked on in indifference.

Stepping next to the couch, L.T. continued to heat the spoon head. "Pull them towels away when I tell you to, wiping as you do," he instructed Marie.

She nodded, repositioning her hands, ready for the call.

"Now!"

Marie slid the towels over Christina's stomach as she pulled them away, just in time as the glowing spoon pressed into the wound.

"Motherfucker!" Christina cried, raising so forcefully she almost broke through Jake and Lilly's restraint. "Fuck me!"

The spoon sizzled into the wound, sending the scent of burning flesh to proliferate the living room. Jake wretched and tucked his head into his shoulder, looking away.

"Ew, gross. That smells like burnt hotdogs," Alex observed, pinching his nose shut.

L.T. pulled the spoon away, looking to see if the cauterization had taken. Satisfied, he said, "Give her another swig, then pour some on that," before walking out of the room to discard the spoon.

Christina took a huge swallow of whiskey and pressed her head back into the couch cushion as Marie doused the forming scab.

"Should be everything you need in that box there to dress it," L.T. said from the doorway, pointing at the coffee table.

Within five minutes, Maria had Christina's wound dressed and wrapped in fresh gauze. Mavid absconded with the remaining whiskey and was now happily rocking on the hall tree, sipping from the bottle every so often.

"She'll be resting for a while," Lilly told everyone. "We need to talk. Preferably outside for a minute."

Jake saw her eyes shift to the three kids sitting on the couch, all three arguing over who was the biggest chicken during Christina's "operation," as they dubbed it.

"Right," Jake confirmed. "You three, stay put. We'll be right back."

As he was walking out of L.T.'s house, Jake heard them protesting, saying if they were old enough to live through the zombie apocalypse, they should have a seat at the big kid's table.

He chuckled.

Don was glad to finally be free from being held captive by the mad school teacher. He'd run as far as he could before his stamina gave out, pausing briefly to catch his breath before continuing down the dirt road. He was at his wits' end with people for the day and wanted to be back home where the world would make sense to him again. No more damsels in distress, no more ladies of the night, no more scissor-wielding basketcases threatening to end his life if he didn't do as they say. No, Don was good with never having to encounter those types of people for the rest of his life. And the fact that those three examples sat in the forefront of his mind, over all the dead folks up and walking around, spoke volumes as he paced himself to a brisk walking speed.

The street he and the Wards lived on was literally across town, and Don hadn't had time to figure out just how he was going to get back there without being attacked by a gang of flesh hungry hoodlums. He figured he could cut through the woods, trespass on the old Foster farm, but he knew it was rough terrain that way, and he was wearing a pair of loafers that weren't built for cross-country.

A gunshot rang out back from the way he'd been fleeing from, causing him to turn and stare down the dirt road. For the briefest of moments, Don considered going back to see what had happened. He tossed the idea into the wind, sharply turning on his heels and continuing on.

Noticing the wind had in fact picked up, carrying with it the heavy stench of decay, Don lamented the fact he didn't have any means to defend himself should a situation arise. A large stick would suffice for now until he was able to find a more suitable weapon, he assured himself.

Pausing and stepping off the road, he searched in the brambles for something that wasn't brittle and would hold up to an attack. As he bent to look, crunching leaves and the snapping of twigs sounded from deeper in the woods. The skin on his arms rippled with fear, and his heart rate began to climb, making his search more manic.

The steady footfalls through the fallen leaves grew louder as they seemed to be heading right for him. Unable to secure so much as a rock, Don dropped to the ground, lying on his stomach, hoping whatever it was hadn't noticed him already and would pass on by without a confrontation.

A sharp pain shot through his ribs, causing him to grunt in pain, as whatever it was tripped over him, crashing onto the forest floor. A white coat came into view as Don rolled over to see what it was, ready to use his fists if it came down to it.

"Doc?" Don asked.

Doc Butler's head popped up, his face grimacing in pain from the fall. "Shelor? That you?"

The two men stared at one another for a moment, dumbstruck by the other's presence so far from the comforts of their natural habitats. Don was first to his feet, angrily brushing away as much dirt from his clothes as he could, before finally offering a hand to help Butler up.

"That you shooting a gun, Don?"

Don shook his head. "No. It came from back that way," he said, motioning with his head.

The doc turned and looked past the bushes for a moment, back down the road where Don had fled from his car. "That's Tierney's place down there, isn't it?"

Still dismayed by his dirty clothes, Don waved a hand in the air dismissively. "Yes. I think so."

"Perfect. Come on," Butler said, walking to the road.

"I don't want to 'come on.' I want to go back home."

Butler looked back at Don for a moment, then down the road in the direction he'd been traveling. "It ain't going to be that way. There's a giant group of... well, whatever they are, and they weren't that far behind me. Been chasing me through the woods all the way from my office," he explained. "Whoever it was firing that gun... Well, that's where we need to be."

Don blew out a heavy breath in a huff. "That's what I was just going over in my head. I could cut through the Foster farm and be home in less than an hour if I really hoofed it."

Doc Butler shook his head and started walking away. "You do what you want, Shelor. But if I was you, I wouldn't go *that* way."

Don stood in the center of the road, jaw clenched, mulling over every option, every possible scenario he could think of. Ideally, going through the property the Foster's had settled their farm on would be the best route to take. And he knew his feet would pay the price. Heading toward Main Street seemed to be one less option now, if Butler was to be believed. Then there was going back to L.T.'s place, and possibly having another run in with Mrs. Nelson—who may or may not be carrying a gun now.

Rocking back on his heels, Don finally caved, calling to the doc.

"Hey, wait up."

"Anybody got the time?" Mavid asked as they all crowded around one of L.T.'s burn barrels.

"Quarter past four," Marie answered after checking her watch.

Jake looked up at the October sky above. "Gonna be getting dark soon. Is your place good to hole up in?" he asked, turning to face L.T.

L.T. shrugged. "Good a place as any, I suppose. I got a lotta supplies stockpiled cause... fuck the government. Don't know how well they'll do with..." L.T. paused a moment as he counted off all of the people currently residing on his property, "...nine people, though."

"Ten," Lilly added, her tone dull, bordering on annoyed. The others all looked around and started to do their own math. "The sheriff is bound to come back at some point," she continued, helping them come to the same conclusion.

"Where is that sumbitch?" Mavid asked, to which no one seemed to hear.

Jake shook his head, disappointed with himself. "Okay, ten people. Surely we can manage ten people for... Well, we don't really know how long this will go on for, but there can't be that many people that were buried around here. Right?"

"Heh. You'd think so, but Lordsland was host to one of the bigger battles during the Civil War. I know for a fact that there were at least three mass graves around these parts. For both sides," L.T. explained.

"Shit, I didn't even think of that. We used to go out to the Foster farm, and Slater Lake, and dig up relics," Mavid pondered.

Lilly spoke up, saying, "I don't remember seeing anyone in a Confederate or Union uniform. And we drove through a lot of those fuckers."

"Yeah, I don't either," Jake added. "Kinda weird, huh?"

Mavid scoffed and then drained the last dregs of L.T.'s expensive whiskey from the bottle he'd been holding, tossing it into the barrel. "This is all fucking weird. I don't know what the rules are for a goddamn zombie apocalypse. All I know is, if we want to have a fighting chance at getting outta here alive, Lance is the man to know."

Marie looked around for a moment, confusion written on her face. "Lance?"

"I think it's the 'L' in L.T., darling," Jake said.

Lilly threw her hands up in the air in frustration. "We need to have a plan in case *more* shit hits the fan."

"What'd ya have in mind?" L.T. asked.

"Guns. Ammo. Whatever you still have around this place to make those dead bastards... deader," Lilly replied.

"Check and check," L.T. said with a grin. "You should know just about everything I got locked in the safe. Might've added a few new toys, here and there. Of course."

Jake looked around the property, willing the cogs in his mind to start turning and formulate some plan of action. His eyes swept over the large military truck that was sitting next to the F-150, before snapping back to the group. "That thing still run?" he asked, turning to face it.

The others around the barrel followed his gaze.

"Like a top," L.T. said, and then laughed heartily.

Shipley left L.T.'s house after telling the others he needed to grab some supplies from his vehicle, and was nearing where he'd left Ramblin' Rose, keeping his peripheral clued in for any movement along the road. He wanted to check the trunk to see if there was a first aid kit in there, and then grab the duffle bag from the passenger seat and take it inside, divvying up what he had, to ensure everyone was able to protect themselves in the event they became overrun with dead folks. Just as he was about to open the door and retrieve the bag, the sound of a man yelling came from further down the road.

The sheriff's hand drew his sidearm quickly and he took aim, waiting to see who it was. He knew they'd left Shelor's car down a little farther back, and Mrs. Nelson lying in the gutter beside it, but to his knowledge, no one else should be this far out Hi-Ho Way that knew better.

Forgetting the duffle bag for a moment, Sheriff Shipley moved down the dirt road, intending to investigate the noise. Shelor's car came into view after a few minutes of walking, the gun held ready to fire should the need arise.

Shipley saw the outline of two people hunched over where the expired teacher lay, but couldn't tell if they were friend or foe. Keeping a safe enough distance between himself and whoever it was, Shipley then noticed the white overcoat one of them was wearing.

"Doc, that you?" he asked, his finger moving to rest on the trigger.

The two that were hunched over rose with a start after hearing the sheriff's question, turning to face the lawman.

"Dan? What in god's name are you doing way out here?" Butler asked.

The tension in Shipley's body lessened after seeing who the pair of unlikely travelers were. "Pick up a stray, did ya?" the sheriff asked, grinning as he tilted his head toward Don.

"So amusing, Shipley. You were always one to make light out of a serious situation. Especially when we were in school," Don spat, sneering at the sheriff.

Shipley ignored the stick in the mud and focused on what the doc had to say.

"Everything's gone to hell in a handbasket, Sheriff. If you haven't noticed," said Butler.

Scratching his brow, Shipley looked around the surrounding woods, nodding in agreement. "Don't I know it, Doc. Whole town's been overrun by dead folks that shouldn't be out and about. Fucked up beyond all recognition is what it is."

Don watched the two men talking, as if a kid that couldn't be included in adult conversation.

"Still, what's got you out here at L.T.'s place? I'd've thought you'd be right in the thick of it. Always been your style."

The sheriff laughed, while Don gave an exaggerated eye roll.

"Normally you'd be right, Doc, but there's a bunch of us that made it out here. We're all up at L.T.'s. Y'all come on up. I think we're going to formulate a plan. Take inventory and regroup," Shipley offered, inclining his head to Don and Butler both.

Doc Butler looked at Don and shrugged. "Still wanting to go it on your own? Or are you going to pull your head out of your ass and be smart about this?"

Don squinted at them, rubbing his hands together in a nervous manner. "Lead the way, oh fearless leader," he answered, shooing them both forward.

Before they could start toward L.T.'s, Shipley paused, spinning around and looking in Don's direction.

"What?" Don asked.

"Shush!" Shipley ordered.

The sheriff closed his eyes and tilted his head sideways. Butler turned, straining his senses. Don stood dumbfounded by their odd behavior until he heard the first inklings of snapping twigs, followed by the mass rustling of leaves.

Turning, Don's mouth fell open in awe. The forest looked like incoming waves of the ocean, lapping onto the shore. Wave after wave of staggering, stumbling corpses moved through the trees, where some fell, others climbed over them in their pursuit of the three nearest, living souls.

"Fuck me." The words fell from Don's slackened mouth without thought.

"Move your asses!" Shipley shouted, grabbing an arm of each man, pulling them out of their stupor.

Don's feet skidded in the gravel but gained traction, leaving Butler and Shipley behind in his trail of dust.

"Huh. I wouldn't have taken those odds in Vegas if I was betting on whether or not Shelor had that kinda speed in him," the doc commented.

"Me neither," Shipley agreed, wasting no time in catching up.

True to L.T.'s word, the old deuce and a half started right up. Despite belching a cloud of black smoke, it smoothed out in a rhythmic purr.

"Always loved this thing," Mavid admitted, running his hand along the olive drab paint. "And when I say she'll go anywhere, I do mean anywhere."

Jake walked to the bed and reached up, pulling on the side railings to test their sturdiness. "L.T., do you have any sheet metal lying around?"

L.T. looked from Jake to the truck, and then back again, thinking before a smile scrolled across his mouth. "I see where you're goin' with this. I think I could rustle somethin' up. Hell, I'll pull the roof off the shed out back... if it comes to that."

Marie had gone back inside to check on the kids and Christina, leaving Lilly to fend for herself with the boys. She climbed into the familiar cab and started adjusting all the mirrors to her liking.

"And what do you think you're doin'?" L.T. asked.

She looked at her ex, her face deadpan. "You and I both know I'm a far better driver than you. Than any of you." Her eyes shifted between Jake, Mavid, and L.T., waiting for one of them to challenge her. When no one did, Lilly's demeanor changed to smug and she continued her personalized adjustments.

"Hey, you've only got a quarter of a tank in this thing. Got any diesel around?"

Again, L.T. thought for a moment. He started to pace back and forth, scratching the back of his neck. "I don't think I have any diesel to put in her, but I might have some old motor oil or something. She'll burn damn near anything you throw in 'er."

Jake considered himself a pretty big history nut, especially when it came to military centric things. It hadn't yet helped in his writing pursuits, but it never stopped him from diving into a deep rabbit hole of research, should the need for the knowledge ever arise. He had about a dozen or so questions he wanted to hurl L.T.'s way, but settled on one—for now.

"This thing ever see action?"

Lilly cut the engine off and hopped down from the cab. "Oh boy, here we go..."

It was L.T.'s turn to roll his eyes at her. "She certainly has! All the way back in Korea."

"Damn," Jake said, surprised. "It looks to be in great shape to be so old."

"Well, me and these two spent an entire summer about... six or seven years back? Fixing it up and restoring 'er to its former glory," Mavid offered, looking like a proud peacock.

"Pshh, I remember you two drinkin' the days away while I was turning wrenches," Lilly scoffed. "I know this gal, inside and out." She gave the truck a loving, motherly look.

L.T. simply shrugged, seeing no fault in her recollection.

Jake shook his head at the two men as he started to walk around the deuce and a half, pulling on different parts here and there. "I think we can make this work for u—"

He quit talking abruptly when he saw movement come from down the driveway. Jogging over to the F-150, Jake pulled out the ax from the back floorboard and gripped it like a baseball bat, ready to strike.

Lilly and Mavid both pulled a gun from their waistbands, taking aim. L.T. remained collected, if not cautious, walking forward to greet who—or what—ever it was.

The approaching shape was coming up faster than Jake had seen any of the zombies in town moving, making him think it wasn't one of the undead. "Is it the sheriff?" he asked.

L.T. held a hand up, indicating for the others to stay back. He knelt next to a nearby tree, coming up with a compound bow in his hands. Nocking an arrow, he drew back, taking aim.

"Friend or foe?" he yelled.

Stopping at the sound of L.T.'s question, eclipsed by the shadows cast by the treetop canopy, the person replied, "Neither," in a breathless cry.

"Is that..." Mavid started.

"Don?" Jake finished, shocked by the man's hustle.

"Y'all know this guy?" L.T. hollered, keeping his sights set on the stranger.

Jake walked forward a few paces, making sure it was really him. Don's chest was heaving as he sucked in air.

"Yeah, that's my neighbor. You alright, Don?" Jake asked.

Don shook his head while swatting the air in front of him. He bent at the waist for a moment, then rose and pointed down the dirt road.

Mavid and Lilly stepped beside Jake, the three of them looking around the struggling man to see what he was trying to convey to them. The sheriff popped into view as he came around the bend, with someone else in tow.

"I do believe that's Doc Butler with Dan," Mavid pondered out loud.

"Yeah, I think you're right. And I think they're bringing a world of shit to our doorstep," Lilly added, her voice holding a slight quiver.

L.T. lowered his bow and looked beyond the two men struggling to move down the driveway, seeing what she was seeing. "Everyone needs to get the fuck inside. NOW!"

Jake was cemented to the spot when he saw a deluge of dead washing over the landscape of the forest. Downtown Lordsland had been bad, but the amount of bodies in the decrepit horde was staggering.

He was stunlocked and his mind failed to function down to the basic levels. All of his worries, of the personal problems he and Marie had been facing, paled in comparison to the hopelessness that flooded in, threatening to drown him faster than water ever could.

Lilly appeared in Jake's view, yelling in his face about something, but his ear failed to hear her words as he went completely numb. The only sense that still seemed to be functioning was his sight.

Jake saw Don run toward him, then disappear. L.T. was picking off the closest threats with his bow—the ones that were bearing down on Shipley and Butler as they were still making their way toward them.

A searing pain jarred Jake out of his stupor, his hand jumping to his cheek where he'd been struck by Lilly.

"Snap the fuck out of it and help me!" she blared at him.

Jake's eyes focused on her and saw the fear she was normally so good at hiding. And he knew if Lilly was scared, they were all fucked.

Lilly growled out in frustration. "Get your ass in the house, old man!" she yelled to Mavid.

Jake looked down at the ax he forgot he was holding, raised it up, and took off toward the sheriff. L.T. released his final arrow, threading it into the eye of one zombie, and then into the slackened mouth of the one behind—dropping them both to the ground, only to be trampled beneath numerous tattered shoes or boney feet.

L.T. tossed his bow to the ground and joined alongside Jake as they raced to aid the two men. Jake heard the deuce and a half fire up behind them, but didn't have time to look back and see what Lilly was up to.

"Get the doc," L.T. told him, pulling a knife from behind his back with his left hand, and taking aim with the pistol in his right.

Jake watched in awe as the man made every bullet count, taking out one of their would-be killers with each shot fired. Raising the ax, he juked past Shipley and Butler, sinking the head into the clavicle of one of the fresher, newly dead. Jake guessed whoever it was hadn't been embalmed, judging by the black, coagulated sludge that poured out from the wound.

Kicking the soulless creature away to free the ax, he backpedaled to avoid the attack of two more that filled the previous one's spot. Jake threw up the handle of the ax to block incoming maws, when L.T. stepped in and slashed at them with his knife, severing one's head completely from its body, and taking off the lower jaw of the other.

"Get them outta here," he commanded Jake, working hard to prevent the wave of undead from attacking the others.

Jake didn't hesitate. He turned and ran for the sheriff and doc, formulating the best way to get them all to safety. He was now able to see what Lilly was doing in the big truck, backing it into the wider area, clipping the big Ford in the process and flipping it onto its side. Shipley and Butler hadn't made it far as Jake caught up to them, grabbing the doc's arm with his free hand to help haul him toward L.T.'s house.

"We ain't gonna make it. Drop me and save yourselves," Butler yelled over the sound of the roaring diesel engine.

"Shut the fuck up and move your ass, old man," the sheriff coughed out, struggling to catch his breath.

Jake caught the fact he, too, was struggling and bore more of the doc's weight. Lilly was coming around with the deuce and a half, barreling right for them.

"What the hell are you doing?" Jake uttered to himself.

Butler looked up and said, "Oh shit!"

The three of them barely had enough time to jump out of the way, leaping to either side of the driveway, as Lilly sped by. Jake landed on the ground with a thud, Butler landing next to him, releasing a grunt that grew into a moan. Flipping over, Jake watched as she steered through the frontline of ghoulish creatures, obliterating them beneath the massive truck. He couldn't find L.T. amongst the mass of bodies, no matter how hard he searched.

The next wave of zombies swarmed the truck, their assault in vain against the sturdy metal. Jake stood and helped Butler to his feet, seeing Shipley was doing the same.

"We need to get to the house," Jake told the doc.

Looking, he saw Mavid standing in the doorway, waving his hand, shouting something Jake couldn't hear over the truck and horde's deathly cries.

Jake shoved the doc away, telling him to go, while he and the sheriff met in the middle of the driveway.

"We need to help," Shipley said.

"How?" Jake asked, looking around but seeing nothing except the wrecked F-150. Squeezing the handle of the ax, he said, "Fuck, I don't know. Something..."

"It's a suicide mission. Get inside... while you still can."

Jake shook his head. "I'm not just going to leave them like this."

Shipley pulled out a handgun and held out a duffle bag for him to take. "Protect the others. Your family."

Looking deep into the sheriff's eyes, Jake knew there was no arguing with the man, and knew he was right. When he begrudgingly took the bag, Shipley walked away, heading for the deuce and a half. Shots started to pop off behind him as Jake jogged for the house.

Butler had just walked inside when Jake met Mavid at the door. "Here. I'm going back to help. They're outnumbered."

Mavid took the bag and tossed it inside the house before grabbing Jake by the arm. "Don't be a goddamned fool. Look."

When Jake looked back down the road, he saw the truck had been completely overtaken by the dead—its engine no longer revving, silent from where he stood.

Shipley was also missing until he scanned the ground and saw a group of ravenous monsters feasting on parts of the lawman, ripping away the uniform he wore in service of Lordsland to get to the tender beneath.

"Come inside, son," Mavid said mournfully, gently tugging on Jake's arm.

Licking his lips before giving in, taking one final look at the setting sun on the horizon, Jake stumbled into the house.

Chapter Ten

C huck Metterelli had been an early riser all his life—and to-day was no different. Sixty-four years—three-hundred and six-ty-five days—worth of sun up to sun down had trained his internal clock to the point of precision. His body was attuned to impending climate changes, and he could tell you when rain was coming by the aches in his knees, and pain in his back. But the storm that swept through the town he was born and raised in last night had him stumped to no end.

"Where was yah magic forecast on this 'un?" May asked as she packed his lunch for the day of hard work in the fields that lay ahead.

Chuck looked at his wife—brow furrowed—but didn't answer her question. They had both woke earlier that morning to the howling winds outside. May was first to her feet, shuffling to the window as she put her slippers on.

"Holy moly, that looks like a damn twista' rollin' through tha hills. Gitcha ass up, we need to head to tha cellar."

She was already throwing her overcoat on by the time Chuck was able to sit up in bed. As he rubbed his eyes, wiping the blurriness out of them, he looked at the clock and saw it was only two in the morning.

"Damnit, woman, ain't had my eight yet. What's got your panties 'a buzzin'?" Chuck asked, looking just in time to dodge out of the way of a flying slipper.

If looks could kill, he'd have been dead in their first year of marriage. Now, in their forty-first, Chuck was used to the daily death-glares his smart mouth earned him.

The windows rattled suddenly, bowing inward and threatening to burst from the outside pressure. Figuring May might've been right about the severity of the situation, Chuck stretched his long john adorned legs and stood, slipping into his own house shoes.

"Come on, then," he urged.

Taking the lead, they traveled down two flights of stairs until the couple reached the root cellar door. Chuck had to shove it open due to the rusted hinges, trying to think when the last time he'd been down here. A face full of cobwebs was his reward for getting the door wide enough for them to squeeze through, spitting out a gob of the dusty silk.

"Yuck," Chuck said as wiped his face clear.

May chuckled at her old fool as she prayed the light still worked before pulling the cord. Though dim, the old bulb lit the cellar enough for them to move a few boxes around and have a place to sit.

The storm raged on around them, battering the house's wall, causing the foundation to groan and protest.

"It'll be a mess to clean up afterwards," May said, and Chuck grunted in agreement.

Three hours lapsed before they heard the last of the wind's mightiness trail off in the distance. Feeling they would be safe to venture above, Chuck stood and went upstairs to check it out. Coming back down, he gave her the all clear.

"Don't bother. I'll have to grease it up, or replace the hinges some other time," he told May as she attempted to close the cellar door behind her.

In the kitchen, May busied herself constructing a lunch for him, knowing he'd be out until late that evening, most likely coming back after the sun had gone down.

She held out the brown paper bag, allowing Chuck a peek inside, his face lighting up when he saw she'd packed a double helping of his favorite.

"Be careful out there today. Drink your water," May advised.

Taking the paper sack, Chuck gave his wife a peck on the lips and said, "Be back in a bit."

Stepping outside, the farm was in disarray; broken limbs and fallen trees lying everywhere. He started making a mental map of how to go about clean up as he strolled toward the barn. Halfway there, May came out onto the porch and called to him.

Chuck turned and saw his wife holding out his hat for him, shaking his head at his forgetful memory.

"Can't go forgettin' that now. My head would look like a tomato by noon," he said, walking back to the house to retrieve it.

Something moved on the porch behind May, and Chuck squinted to figure out what it was. She must've heard it because she turned away from him to look, then yelled from whatever it was she saw. As May fell to the porch—overtaken by something—Chuck dropped the paper sack on the ground and jogged as fast as his knees would allow.

"Dear lord," he said after seeing his wife covered in blood from a gaping wound in her neck.

The monster—the only way Chuck could describe it in his mind—looked up at him, its dried out eye sockets boring into him.

The thing abandoned his wife, moving to the porch railing and toppled over the top. Chuck backed up, keeping his eyes locked onto whatever it was. From the flowerbed, it rose on two legs, and he realized it was a person that attacked his wife. What stood out to Chuck were the clothes it was wearing. A tattered red flannel shirt, filthy blue jeans that were hard to distinguish their original color, and a set of old, worn work boots that Chuck knew all too well.

"D-Daddy?" he stuttered, questioningly.

The thing ignored Chuck's question; freshly churned soil clinging to its face, giving it a fuller look where the rest of its body looked emaciated beyond comprehension. Reaching for him, Chuck swatted his deceased father's hand away and turned, headed for the porch where May lay, bleeding out.

Fumbling up the stairs, Chuck paused for a brief moment as he saw the life draining out of his wife, spreading across the wooden planks of the old porch. The former patriarch of the Metterelli family was hot on his son's heels, grabbing at Chuck's waist, threatening to drag the old man down next to May.

Cocking his leg forward then driving it back behind him, Chuck felt the sole of his boot connect with something and the hold on him released. With a quick glance back, he saw his daddy's head had left his body and was rolling across the ground as the rest of the corpse collapsed.

Rushing to May's side, Chuck instantly saw he was too late to do anything to help. Her once beautiful blue eyes stared unknowing at the side of the house, the life that had filled them was now gone.

He wailed as he scooped her into his arms, pulling the only woman he'd ever truly loved to his chest, praying for a miracle.

"Please, Lord... Please give me back mah May. I'll do anything. Just let me have her back for a little while longer. I-I... I didn't even get to tell 'er bye..."

Chuck openly wept as he continued to hold her and pray. Silent tears shed and silent prayers sent, but he couldn't bring himself to look down at her pale face. At the finality of the fate of every living creature.

And then she stirred.

May began to twitch in his arms like a stretching kitten, arms and legs stiffening before relaxing again. When Chuck finally looked down at his wife, her eyes looked back at him, but a milky film was now covering them, blotting out the rich blue.

"M-May? Are y-you really bac—ack!!"

Chuck jerked in pain as he felt her teeth sink into his pecks through his shirt, clamping down and tearing a chunk out when he pushed her head away. Her teeth clacked together repeatedly—new spurts of blood issuing from the hole in her neck with each snap—attempting to take another bite, so he held her off by palming her forehead.

"May, stop! What are you doing? What's wrong with you?" Chuck asked, his voice cracking.

As if she didn't hear his pleas, Chuck's wife continued her attacks, relentlessly seeking his flesh, gnashing and spitting.

May's hands came up, her fingernails digging into Chuck's face. He tried to shake them off, but couldn't get far enough away and still hold her snapping maw at bay.

He screamed as she started to peel away the skin of his cheeks and forehead, digging deeper into the meat of his face.

"May, goddoggit. Stop!"

Chuck grabbed a handful of his wife's hair and yanked her head to the side, hearing a loud crack and watched as she went limp in his arms, once again.

The shock of what he'd done crashed over his senses all at once, and he howled like a lone wolf would toward the moon.

It was two in the afternoon when Chuck finished digging the double grave—reburying his father, and now interring his wife under the old oak tree behind the house.

Digging was hard enough trying to get past the root system, but every so often, he'd have to stop after another dead relative would wander up to where he was working. After quickly dispatching the corpse with the pick he was using, Chuck covered the grave under the tree and paid a visit to the family cemetery near the edge of the property. Upturned soil, bones, and a few animated bodies littered the ground. A few of them had gotten stuck clawing their way to the surface, their limbs either breaking in the process, or were too entangled with something below the topsoil, out of Chuck's view.

Most of the ones that were entombed he'd never actually met in person, only hearing their names through reminiscences from his dad or uncles, so when Chuck ended their new lease on life, he didn't feel much of anything aside from the reverberation through pick handle as he drove it through the tops of their skulls.

Nothing made sense to Chuck anymore. Not since being woken up in the middle of the night to a rampaging tornado outside, later to have his wife killed by his dead father, then come back to life and try and attack him, to which he, himself, had to put an end to.

But Chuck was a simple man, with simple values, and without May by his side any longer, he had nothing left at all.

As he made his way back to the front of the house, he saw the brown paper bag he'd abandoned earlier. Bending to pick it up, Chuck retrieved one of the sandwiches from within—the last meal his May would ever fix him—and unwrapped it. Savoring the bologna and cheese on white, he looked out at the edge of the distant pasture and saw a group of bedraggled looking folks meandering around.

Never one to think outside the box much, Chuck suspected there was a good chance that the dead rising from their graves wasn't as localized to his farm as he thought. His initial plan for tackling the downed trees and limbs seemed just a valid solution in this situation as any. Rolling the paper bag closed as he finished the sandwich, he tucked it under his arm as he strolled to the barn where he kept his farming equipment.

May had been highly displeased when he brought the giant machine home late one evening. But after working a few jobs for the township of Lordsland, she finally came around to seeing the utility of having such a contraption on hand.

Settling into the cab of the HOG trimmer, Chuck tucked the brown bag next to him, saving the last sandwich for later. Turning the key, the machine purred to life.

Often, Chuck would make clever puns or jokes about how useful his HOG was, or how big it was. More often than not, May would roll her eyes and ignore the bait he was dangling, but on rare occasions, he'd catch her falling for it and relish in the giggle she'd unknowingly let slip out.

This instrument panel lit up like a Christmas tree with no indicators of malfunction. Engaging the transmission, Chuck steered the HOG out of the dim barn, into the bright sunlight. Turning back toward the field, more decrepit bodies had joined the smaller group he'd seen earlier.

Raising the tri-blade, Hover Over Ground cutting system, Chuck said, "Let's git'r done," and flipped the switch to engage the spinning action. The blades whirled to life, creating a hum that filled the cab. Turning toward the field, Chuck accelerated head-on, leveling the cutting apparatus to about five feet above the ground.

The noise from the HOG must have attracted the attention of the wanderers because their focus was now drawn to him. Stopping midway across the pasture, Chuck eased on the brake, holding steady on the spot while he observed the undead group.

One by one, they walked head-first into the spinning blades with no concern of self-preservation. He'd expected as much, but wanted to be sure and test his theory before going on some kind of wild killing spree of people that weren't actually dead.

The HOG held up its end of the bargain, shredding up the mindless fools into human confetti without a bit of trouble. Pressing on, Chuck directed the newly christened machine of death's destruction to the few stragglers that hadn't been in a hurry to die a second time and mowed them down to the ground.

After disengaging the blades and guiding the HOG back to the house, Chuck started down the farm's long driveway, pausing for a moment before moving onto the blacktop. He turned in the seat and looked at the old family homestead in the distance.

Every fiber of his being told him he would never see home again after leaving, and without May being there to greet him on the porch after a day working the fields, it wasn't home any longer, anyway. Not anymore.

Clearing his throat—and mind—of emotions, Chuck hit the pavement wide open, spotting a handful of undead up ahead. Re-engaging the cutting system, he forged on. To whatever end.

Chapter Eleven

J ake fell to the floor of L.T.'s house, startling the three kids to their feet. Mavid—who'd been standing by the door—attempted to get him to his feet, but was shrugged off by him, Jake telling the old man to give him a minute.

Marie dropped to her knees in front of her husband, Alex stepping in behind her. "What is it?" she asked, gently lifting his head by the chin to look into her eyes.

"Th-they're..." Jake looked up and saw the fear written on Alex's face. His gaze wandered to the others in the room and saw the same look on their faces reflected back at him. "...gone."

Doc Butler threw himself into a chair, covering his face with his hands, while Don paced the floor, muttering to himself incoherently.

Alex kneeled beside Jake and buried his head into his dad's shoulder. Marie wrapped her arms around the two of them, squeezing them tightly. Looking past his wife's shoulder, he saw Christina was still unconscious on the couch.

"Hey, Doc. Can you see to her? She was stabbed in the gut."

Butler wiped at his face and cleared his throat. "Yeah... of course."

"I'll lend a hand, too," Mavid offered, leaving the Wards to tend to one another. "You two, come on. Maybe you'll learn something." Mavid ushered Rachel and Spike toward the couch.

Without warning, the walls of the house shook all at once, a cacophony of thunderous pounding coming inward from outside. Jake felt Alex start to shake in his arms and rubbed his son's back, telling him they were alright.

"We need to figure out what to do next." Marie had to raise the lever of her voice to be heard.

"I know. I just don't know what. We're surrounded on all sides. Nowhere to run."

Marie eased her hug around the two of them and leaned back. "Then we stand our ground. We fight until we can't. What other choice do we have?"

It was Alex that answered. "We can do this, Dad. I've done it thousands of times before."

Jake couldn't help the smile that spread over his face. "This isn't a video game, bud. This is real life. No cheat codes for what we're up against."

Alex nodded he understood, but Jake could see the determination written in his eyes. Patting his son on the shoulder, Jake felt he was able to stand again and wanted to see what the doc's assessment of Christina was.

As he walked across the living room, he took a moment to address Don. "Don? Don?! How are you holding up?"

Don stopped pacing and looked at Jake, his eyes crazed, unable to remain locked on any single thing, as if he was frantically searching for something. "Ward? Right, right... of course you're here." Don looked around the room. "And with your family. That's..." Don left the rest of his sentence hanging in the air and went back to pacing around the room.

To see his neighbor—no matter how he'd felt about the man in the past—so disheveled and out of sorts, shook Jake a little. In his mind,

Don had been the epitome of collected—to a fault and the reason why they'd butted heads so often. Making a mental note to circle back around and see if there was a way to snap him out of it, Jake moved on to the couch.

"What are you thinking, Doc?"

Butler was sitting on the coffee table, leaning over Christina as he checked her over. "Who did the cauterization?" he asked.

"I think it was L.T. and Lilly that handled it," Mavid said.

"Hmmm, what'd they use?"

"Big spoon and a torch, I believe it was."

Butler nodded and then shrugged. "They did a pretty damn good job from what I can tell. She's sleeping, for now. Let her."

"We need to make a plan and act fast."

Jake looked at Spike and Rachel who were holding their hands over their ears to help muffle the sound of the rotten limbs slapping the outside of the house.

Mavid leaned in close to Jake and said, "Don't you think we should do it somewhere a little more... private?"

Jake turned and found Alex, who was standing close by, and pulled him in to stand in front of him. "No, I do not. We're all in this together."

Mavid tilted his head to the side and smirked. "Aye. 'Spose you're right."

"You probably know L.T.'s place better than any of us. Do you know where he'd keep stuff that would help us out? Weapons, guns, anything that we'd be able to defend ourselves with..."

Mavid thought for a moment then nodded. "Be right back," he told them as he disappeared down the hallway.

"What's next?" Marie asked.

"We need to make sure they can't get in through the windows and stuff," Spike offered.

Jake looked at the boy, impressed with his input. "Exactly. Whatever you can find. Tables, bookcases, shelves... Make sure we get the doors and windows blocked so they can't get in. You three think you can handle that?"

Spike, Rachel, and Alex all said they could and went to work, moving whatever they could over the potential entrance points.

After he saw the kids' attention was focused on the task, Jake huddled with Marie. "Don... Can you do something with him? I think he's cracked or something. See if you can settle him down, or bring him around to a right frame of mind."

Marie licked her lips. "I can try. What are you going to do?"

Jake took her hands in his and gave them a squeeze, seeing her wince. Looking down, he saw the bandages were fully saturated with blood that had crusted over.

"Have Butler take a look at those, and rewrap them. I'm going to see if there is a way up onto the roof from the inside. That's our Alamo if things take a turn for the worse."

"Gotcha," she replied. Before he was able to let go, she pulled him close. "Jake, I... I'm sorry. I lov—"

"I know, Marie. I know."

Before another word could pass between them, they both met in the middle, their lips pressing together in a quivering kiss.

"I'll be back in a minute," Jake said before walking away.

"Don, Doc, join me at the kitchen table for a moment, please," Maire requested.

Lilly laid in the cab of the deuce and a half, watching as reanimated corpses blotted out any ambient light coming in from the outside, creating a faux night inside the truck. The second the horde had swarmed in, she tried to maneuver the awkward old Army vehicle through the sea of bodies, but a loud clunk sounded from beneath the truck—the axle snapping—so she took cover in the floorboard.

It had been a suicide mission, Lilly knew that when she ran to the truck in the first place, but when she saw L.T. running head-first into danger, her mind turned off and instinct took over. Despite the differences they had in the past, he had been a huge part of her life and she still cared for the man, though she'd never admit it to a living soul.

Lilly's one hope—as she listened to the skittering of dead things clamor around her—was that her sacrifice wasn't in vain. That everyone had been able to get safely inside before being overrun. Especially L.T.

Settling in for a long, drawn out death—or miracle—Lilly pondered whether she possessed the ability to take a nap through the rocking motion created by the dead jostling into the sides of the truck. Doubtful that she would be able to, Lilly held to the notion that out of sight, out of mind was the best course forward. At least for now.

After Jake asked if he could secure them some weapons, Mavid had a good idea where he'd be able to find something, if L.T. still had his bunker stocked. Walking into the master bedroom, Mavid closed the door behind him before pulling up on the mattress of the queen-sized bed. A hatch was revealed, perfectly situated in the middle of the bed frame that would be invisible to anyone not in the know.

Grunting as he twisted the handle, he was able to crack the seal after putting a little elbow grease into it. Flipping a switch just inside the portal, Mavid saw a string of lights below come to life. Taking a deep breath, he descended the ladder into the bunker below.

Mavid couldn't recall the last time he'd visited L.T.'s end of days contingency, but his friend had been busy by the looks of things. Big stacks of crates lined the walls that hadn't been there previously, all labeled as food stuffs. Cases of bottled water sat atop the crates, enough to last a single person months if Mavid was to wager a guess. A cot, cookstove, and wash basin sat in the corner, all the amenities a person would need while trying to survive the apocalypse.

"God doggy. You done planned for something, didn't ya?"

Moving around in the small space, Mavid had to admire L.T.'s ingenuity. Though compact, and stocked to the brim, it didn't feel claustrophobic to him. Skirting along the crates, Mavid spotted what he'd come for. A large gun safe sat in the corner opposite of the cot, with an electronic keypad that would open it.

Swiping his hand over his face, Mavid knew his memory wasn't what it used to be, but that didn't matter in this case. He knew exactly the right numbers to key in to gain access.

"Oh-nine. Twenty-four. Eighty-six."

A click sounded inside and the door popped ajar. "You old sappy sumbitch," he said, grinning as he shook his head.

Pulling the door open, Mavid's eyes went wide when he saw the stockpile of weapons. Reaching in, he grabbed a set of AK-47s and propped them against the crates next to him. A large satchel of magazines hung on a hook, and after checking the caliber, he pulled it out as well. There were at least thirty other guns inside, most looked to be fully automatic rifles—likely unregistered if he knew L.T.—along with a few handguns sitting on an upper shelf.

Grabbing the .44 magnum and stowing it in the waistband of his pants at the small of his back, Mavid also picked up a couple 9mm pistols, as a last resort if it came down to it.

Looking around, he grabbed one of the pillows off the cot and shucked the pillowcase off, planning to use it as a tote. Dumping in the handguns, magazines, and a bottle of Jack Daniels that was sitting conveniently next to the cot, Mavid shouldered the rifles and walked to the ladder.

Staring up to the bedroom above, a few thoughts occurred to him. First being that no one else in the house knew of the hidden bunker. He could simply seal the hatch and live like a king for the rest of his days, however few those would be.

The second, and less evil in his eyes, was to coral everyone down into the bunker and wait out the storm. But to Mavid, it was hard to see the worth in a slow, drawn out death as they all starved, or died of thirst.

Looking up the ladder, the options weighed heavily on his mind. Opening the pillowcase, he thought a little whiskey might help make things more clear.

Alex held the coffee table up to the window as Spike and Rachel pushed a recliner against it to hold it in place. The three of them had taken the task of securing all windows and doors seriously. They hadn't decided whether to use the couch to blockade the door, or one of the larger shelves.

"Did either of you check to make sure the door was actually locked?" Rachel asked, to which Spike and Alex looked at one another and shrugged.

She scoffed before walking over to the front door and tested it, finding that it was indeed unlocked. Shaking her head, Rachel turned the switch to lock it, and then threw the deadbolt in place as well.

Scratching sounds could be heard from outside, and she saw there was a peephole. Going to her tippy toes, she peered through and and jerked her head back.

"That's disgusting."

"Lemme see!" Spike rushed to the door and looked, twisting up his face in revolt.

Curiosity got the better of Alex and he, too, looked through the peephole to see what was on the other side. A single eye could be seen through the fisheye glass, drooping out of its socket. Half of the corpse's head was missing, jagged fragments of skull poking through papery-thin skin, with matted hair plastered in the crater.

Alex drew back and mimicked like he was going to barf on the other two.

"Ew! Stop!" Rachel cried.

Spike laughed and then took another look. "This is even better than that one game..."

Alex saw Rachel roll her eyes and turn toward the couch. "Help me with this."

Together, they scooted the heavy piece of furniture until it was firmly against the door, nearly pinning Spike before he hopped over it and helped.

Looking around the living room, Alex was satisfied with their makeshift fortifications. "What's next?"

Spike mounted the back of the couch and continued gawking outside.

"Living room is pretty safe, I guess. I don't think we should go into the kitchen at the moment," Rachel said.

Alex looked through the doorway and saw his mom having a hushed conversation with Don and Doc Butler. He agreed with Rachel's assessment and shrugged. "Let's hang out until my dad gets back. He'll know what to do next."

With most of the furniture being used as barricades, he motioned for her to join him on the floor next to the couch Christina was still asleep on. Alex saw a slight frown on her face as she dropped to sit next to him.

"I'm so tired. It feels like it's been days since all this started." Rachel yawned, as if to accentuate her point.

"Right? And who knows when all this shi... all this will end."

Alex looked up at an old cuckoo clock on the wall—desperately in need of repair as one of the yellow birds that would normally be perched at the top was hanging upside down—and saw it was nearly eleven. On a normal day, this was a school night and he'd have already been in bed for an hour. He doubted there would be school tomorrow, or the rest of the week—especially since their teacher was lying dead in a ditch down the driveway somewhere. Alex didn't know what life would be since zombies were now walking the earth, but given present company, he couldn't complain much.

"What is it?"

"Huh?"

"You've got a weird, happy look on your face." Rachel raised her eyebrows as she waited for an answer.

"Oh," Alex felt his cheeks start to burn, "I was just thinking, I don't guess there will be school tomorrow."

Rachel giggled, which caused Alex to laugh.

Feeling his hand slide on something that was peeking out from underneath the couch, Alex picked up a sheet of paper, unable to make heads or tails of what it was referring to about some kind of ritual, and balled it up before tossing it into the empty waste bin next to the couch.

Their attention was drawn to the front door when they heard knocking. Looking, Spike was rapping his knuckles against the wood to the tune of A Shave and a Haircut, and then waited for a return knock before trying again.

"What are you doing," Alex asked.

Spike turned to look at them. "I want to see how smart they are. Would be good to know if they still had some of their memories."

Again, he knocked. And again, it went unanswered.

"Cut it out, fool." Alex shook his head at his friend, wondering if he actually knew anything about how zombified people worked.

Ignoring him, Spike continued the call sign.

Marie ushered Butler and Don into the kitchen, pulling out a chair, insisting Don sit for a moment. The naturally reluctant man remained standing until the doc placed a hand on his shoulder and gently, but firmly, pushed him into the seat. Marie took the other seat at the small table, while the doc pulled over the step-stool and sat between them.

"What's going on, Don?" she asked.

Don's eyes darted around the kitchen, seemingly unable to lock onto anything and remain focused. Butler and Marie shared a look.

Rubbing his chin, Butler asked, "Hey, Don, would you mind if I looked you over for a moment? You know, just to make sure you're not hurt or anything?"

Don nodded. Butler looked around and grabbed a pen that was sitting on the table. Holding Don by the chin, he instructed the man to follow the pen with his eyes without moving his head. After that test, the doc administered a few others while Marie looked on.

"Don," Butler started, "I think you're suffering from shock."

"What can we do to help, Doc?" Marie asked.

Butler pulled his mouth to one side and spoke in a low voice. "Well, s'far as I can tell, he's physically fine, so this must be emotional shock from everything that's been going on. We could lay him down for a while and see if he snaps out of it."

"I'm not going to lay down. I'm fine."

Marie and Butler's heads both snapped over to Don, whose face held his normal, stern sneer like something close by smelled bad.

"Well... alright then," Butler replied. "Are you really 'fine'?"

Staring directly into the doc's eyes, Don said, "Yes. Now what's going on? Where am I?"

Marie took in a deep breath, ready to explain everything.

Jake walked down the same hallway Mavid had, closing any doors he found to still be open in hopes of adding another hurdle for the dead folks outside, just in case they happened to get in. Before he made it to the end of the corridor, where a final door stood already closed, he looked up and saw exactly what he'd been searching for.

Reaching up, Jake pulled on the cord that would bring down a ladder leading up to the attic. Unfolding the sectioned steps, he partially climbed up and looked around—checking to see if the coast was clear—before continuing the rest of the way.

A pull cord hung down from above and Jake pulled it to illuminate the dark recesses of the attic. The space was small and stuffy, with boxes piled up haphazardly along the rafters. A small, vented window was set in the wall toward the front of the house, too small to make for an easy escape route for any of them from what Jake could tell.

Slowly making his way to the window, he was careful not to step on the insulation in between the trusses. A sea of bodies shambled around L.T.'s yard, seemingly unending as they filtered through the trees around the property. He looked in either direction, trying to find a route out of here.

Having already known it, Jake still couldn't help himself as he said, "We're fucking surrounded on all sides."

The stench of death hung heavily in the air as it filtered in from the outside. Jake could see the moon peeking out through the clouds as it crept across the sky. He didn't know how long the house would keep them safe, or if there was any way out of the corner they'd pinned themselves in.

Something in the distance caught his ear, a low humming over the moans and groans below he couldn't quite place. Someone on the floor below him yelled something inaudible, but they must've been seeing the same thing he was.

Tiny light beams in the distance broke up through the trees, casting long, tall shadows over the forest. The humming grew louder, the lights larger, as whatever it was steadily charged toward the house.

Jake repositioned himself at the small window as he watched from above. The horde of zombies started to turn and face whatever the large machine heading their way was. A spark of hope lit in his heart that maybe his prayers had been answered. Whoever was driving that thing, he'd lay a big, sloppy kiss on them when they met.

The hum grew to a steady whirl, intermixed with a grinding sound as the front of the machine raised and lowered. Awestruck by the genius of using such a thing to exterminate the scourge that had befallen Lordsland, Jake watched as, one by one, the dead walked into their ultimate demise.

Chuck had spent the day carving a path through town, cutting down small pockets of reanimated corpses until he reached Main Street. There, the crowd thickened, creating a near impassable blockade of rotting flesh had he been in a regular vehicle. Keeping the blades engaged, Chuck continued at a leisurely pace, watching as ruined remains were flung out on either side of the HOG.

As he neared the edge of town, just at the edge of the parking lot of Doc Butler's office, Chuck saw that a slew of the dead folks had splintered off and were heading down the road toward Pleasant Ridge Cemetery.

Reaching up and flipping on the headlights in the dusky evening sunset, he took a hard right, opting to follow the crowd.

Again, as he approached the next intersection, the long line of dead folks diverged from the natural path of the road and headed down Hi-Ho Way—as if marching with a purpose.

Shrugging to himself, Chuck followed the flow of bodies and took the HOG off the pavement and headed down the dirt road.

The rocking motion lulled Chuck as his thoughts wandered to May. His stomach grumbled and he remembered the sandwich he'd stashed earlier. First pulling it from the paper bag, then shucking off the plastic wrapping, he sank his teeth in, savoring every morsel.

And what a fine, last meal this is, Chuck thought and took another bite.

Easing off the accelerator, Chuck saw a car blocking the road up ahead. He circumnavigated it, lowering the cutting blades to cut out the thick brush alongside the road. It was hard to see in the dark, but Chuck didn't think he recognized the car sitting there, and wondered what the story behind it was.

Back on the dirt road, he drew close to the driveway and saw another, larger vehicle sitting in the way. The living dead things were crawling over it with decrepit bodies, writhing on the cab like a knot of worms trying to untangle themselves. Chuck steered to the right of the big truck, cutting a path through the corpses that were standing around, turning to the left to see if there was anyone inside.

A shriek of metal on metal rang out and the HOG came to a shuttering stop, causing him to drop the half-eaten sandwich and lurch forward against the steering wheel. A shower of sparks shot out from the cutting head and he tried to raise the boom arm that was now stuck on something.

"Dagnabit!" he cried, throwing the transmission into reverse.

The HOG stayed where it was and he rose from his seat to see what he was hung on. A newer looking truck was lying on its side, and the cutter apparatus was now entangled in its undercarriage. Plopping back down, Chuck disengaged the blades, watching as the numerous, necrotized bodies started to mount the HOG.

Just before his view was blocked, Chuck saw silhouettes moving in the house up ahead.

Lilly heard the sound approaching from the floor of the deuce and a half and wondered who would be out mowing at night—in the apocalypse, no less. Rising, she saw brief slivers of light through the gaps in between bodies, hearing the sound of human mulch being made.

Seeing the large machine crash into the F-150, Jake groaned as he watched the driver attempt to unfuck their fuck up, then heard the whoosh of the blades cut off.

"Fuck. Fuck. Fuck."

Stepping back—his mind failing to remember his surroundings—his foot hit a soft patch of insulation, throwing his balance off as he fell back through the ceiling, crashing into the living room below.

"What the hell was that?" Christina asked, snapping awake and speaking before anyone else could react.

The fall had knocked the breath out of him, but Jake rolled over, shaking off the shock of the impact.

"Are you okay, Dad?" Alex asked, rushing to his side.

Jake nodded his head, still not able to intake a full breath. Marie rushed in from the kitchen, accessing him for injuries.

"...fi... 'm fine."

Sucking in air, Jake rose on all fours, working up to standing when he felt able.

"Meeerrrrrrryyy Christmas, motha truckers!" Mavid announced as he re-entered the living room holding a small arsenal.

"Woah! Are those real?" Spike asked.

"Wouldn't be much good if they weren't," Mavid replied with a grin. "Now, who wants one?"

"Hell yeah!"

Mavid pulled back the AK-47 he was holding out when Spike rushed toward it with outstretched hands. Giving the boy a stern look, the old man said, "Adults only for anything that has a trigger. I don't need my ass getting shot off by a kindergartener."

Rachel giggled at the slight as Spike puffed up his chest. "I'm eleven, you big old geezer."

Jake couldn't help but laugh as Marie helped him to his feet. Don and Butler joined everyone in the living room.

Christina moaned and held her side. "Anyone got a drink? Smack, ice, smoke? I'd take anything really."

Doc Butler cleared his throat. "Best to keep your wits about you. Especially if guns are in play.

"Guns?" Christina looked around the room and then spotted Mavid. "Where is my gun? Did someone grab it?"

When no one spoke up, she shook her head. "Do you know how many beej's I had to give for that?"

"Alright," Marie cut in, "What's the plan? How are we going to get out of here in one piece? All of us."

Mavid walked over to the coffee table Jake had miraculously missed in his fall and laid out the rifles and handguns he'd brought up from the bunker.

"Adults only," he reiterated, scrunching up his face at Spike and sticking out his tongue.

After Jake, Marie, Don, and Butler were armed, Christina still pouting that no one had retrieved her pistol after she'd killed Mrs. Nelson, Jake walked over to the front-facing window and looked out around the makeshift fortification.

"Whoever it is driving that thing took out a lot of them. With the guns, we might be able to go out and rescue the driver. Or untangle the mower and take out the rest of them. That'd be our best bet, I think."

No one objected, or interjected a better idea. It was decided Jake and Mavid would be the ones to go out on the rescue mission, while Butler and Don stood watch at the door, providing cover fire when necessary.

After Mavid gave Jake a quick tutorial on how to operate the guns—"Just point and pull the damn trigger, it'll do the rest" —Marie pulled Jake to the side.

"Are you sure about this? I... I don't want to lose you twice in one day." Her eyes fell to the floor in shame.

"That machine is our best bet. Someone out there, who risked their life, is trapped inside with no way to do anything. It's the least we can do for them."

When Marie looked back up at him, he could see her eyes were now moist. Jake reached up and brushed away a single tear that was threatening to fall.

"Keep everyone safe in here. Make sure none of the dead get inside."

She nodded and started to turn before he stopped her and pulled her in close, planting his lips on hers.

"I'll be back in a minute," Jake said.

Before she could reply, a scream echoed from outside. Everyone except Christina rushed to the window to look out and see what was going on.

Stepping away, Marie reached in her pocket. "It's dark out there, take these," she said, holding out a couple of flashlights. Mavid and Jake each took one.

"You ready to go, old man?" Mavid nodded and took a long pull from a bottle of whiskey.

"Let's go!" Jake said as he scooted the couch away from the front door.

Charging a round into the chamber of the rifle, Jake clicked on the flashlight and pulled the door open.

Chapter Twelve

Lilly was able to get a better idea of what was going on when the zombies that had been blocking her windows were drawn to whatever the machine had been. Looking out the back glass of the truck, it was still too dark to tell exactly what it was, but bet everything she had it was Chuck Metterelli and his fancy brush hog. Though he was never a patron of hers at McGoo's, he'd stopped in a few times while driving it around town, inviting anyone that feigned interest to come out for a full breakdown of all the glorified weed eater's features.

She noticed the herd around her was thinned significantly, and decided to try and start the engine. Sending out a silent prayer to whatever god or omnipotent, divine beings pulled all the strings in the universe, Lilly turned the key in the ignition and felt her stomach drop when nothing happened.

"Not even a click. Fuck my life."

She had to laugh at her own words, thinking that's exactly what was happening. She was fucked and, as always, it was up to her to unfuck it.

Looking around the moonlit cab of the deuce and a half, she couldn't find anything that would help her defend herself if need be. Reaching behind the bench seat, her hand found something in the dark and she pulled it up and over, unable to comprehend why L.T. had had a golf club stashed in the old truck.

"It's not nothing," she said to herself, sizing up the long, slender shaft of metal.

Her knowledge of the sport of golf was less than none, but judging by the large head of the club, Lilly had no doubt she'd be able to bash some brains in if it came down to it.

Hearing Chuck's machine shrieking behind her then cutting off, she turned and squinted into the gloom, its headlights barely piercing the darkness to cast a dim glow on the front of the house.

Building up her courage, Lilly took a deep breath before throwing the truck door open, leaping to the ground and instantly losing her footing in the slimy slush.

Not having time to worry about what it was, she struggled to her feet, slipping and finding it hard to gain traction, using the club to remain upright.

Though the cutter was turned off, Lilly could hear the engine of the brush hog still idling as she got closer. She could see bodies crawling over every part of it and wondered if Chuck was still alive inside.

Cautious in her approach, shadows seemed to move within shadows so Lilly swung the golf club, unable to tell what was real and what her mind was projecting to be there.

On her third swing, the club connected with something and she felt it go down to the ground.

"This is fucked. I can't see a goddamn thing!" Her lungs seared as she took in deep breaths.

Coming up to the back of the brush hog, Lilly banged the club on the engine compartment, trying to draw the attention of the ones attempting to get in where the operator sat. None of the dead paid her any mind, determined to get into the cab.

Lilly started to scream as loud as she could, finally gaining the ire of the ones closest by.

"Heh, didn't exactly think this one through," she said aloud as she backed away until hitting something hard enough to knock her off her feet.

From the house, she looked as she heard gunfire ring out.

Jake shone the light in front of him as he stepped out into L.T.'s front yard. The darkness outside of the beam was oppressive and gave him chills, not knowing what was out there. He felt Mavid brush past him, stalking straight from the large machine near the overturned truck.

"Hey, stay together!" Jake called harshly.

Whether he heard him or not, Mavid paid no mind, popping off a few rounds from his rifle. Whatever had been in that bottle, Jake wondered if he had anymore. Following the old man's lead, Jake nervously held his own rifle out in front of him.

Mavid continued to fire selective shots as they got closer to where the machine sat idling. The face of an expired person appeared in between the two, catching Jake off guard as he fumbled to find the trigger with his finger.

"Christ!" he yelled, stepping back as the thing's soulless eye sockets bore into him with malice.

Jake lunged to the right, finally able to correct the rifle, and took aim where a nose would've been on a living person. Pulling the trigger, the rifle bucked against his shoulder while the flash from the muzzle momentarily blinded him. As his vision readjusted to the dimness of the flashlight, Jake saw his shot was true and there was now a headless body lying on the ground in front of him.

Possibly for the first time in his life, he felt power like he never had before. Jake shook off any hesitations he'd had about the use of guns and took aim again as another corpse came into the light.

As before, the rifle recoiled and another decapitated body added itself to the growing number that littered the ground.

Looking, he saw Mavid was already at the machine, clearing out a path to get to whoever was inside. Jake took aim and took out two skeletal walkers that were coming up behind the old man with a series of burst shots. Closing the gap between him and Mavid, Jake scanned the area around the machine and stopped, not believing what he was seeing. There, huddled on the ground, and holding what looked like a golf club, was Lilly.

Bypassing where Mavid was still taking out a slew of zombies with relative ease, Jake rushed to Lilly. Sliding in the fallen leaves, he went to his knees and brought the flashlight up to check and make sure she was still alive.

"Hey, hey! Please tell me you're alright." Jake pleaded with desperation.

"What the fuck took you so long?" Lilly replied, looking up at him.

He released a deep sigh of relief and dropped the rifle, pulling her to his chest, wrapping her in his arms.

"Yeah, I, uh, missed you, too," she said.

Backing off, Jake looked at her and said, "I... we all thought you were dead."

"I feel dead. Help me u—"

Lilly was cut off by a growing howl in the distance. They looked around, trying to find where it was coming from. Through the trees, high on a distant hill, Jake saw the source and could not comprehend it.

Backdropped by the newly waning moon, air whipped into a twirling cyclone, pulling in all manner of matter within its suctional reach.

"Oh, fuck," they said in unison.

Jake dragged Lilly to her feet, his rifle and her golf club left forgotten on the ground. Shining the flashlight, he found Mavid standing next to the large machine, changing out the magazine of his rifle—a pile of bodies mounded up around him.

"Oh, hey, Lil," he said as they reached him.

"Hey yourself, old man. We need to get the fuck out of here," she yelled.

As if to punctuate her point, forceful gusts of wind blasted all three of them from every direction. Taking his rifle, Mavid tapped on the door to get the attention of the driver.

The door of the cab opened and an old man with shaggy silver hair and wearing bib overalls poked his head out. "Yeah?" he asked.

"You just gonna sit in there all night, Chuck? Or are you gonna do something with that thing?" Mavid asked.

Struggling to keep the door open against the wind, Chuck looked toward the front of the machine and nodded. "Hung up on that dagum truck."

Lilly scoffed. "Leave it and get your ass inside before we're all sucked into oblivion!"

Jake saw the old man's face go slack at the suggestion of abandoning his rig.

"Ain't gonna happen. Plus, how are you gonna get back in there with all them blocking the way?"

Three heads turned as Jake and Mavid raised their flashlights to find a wall of corpses standing between them and the front door to L.T.'s house.

"How are there so many fucking dead people in this town?!" Jake shouted, half drowned out by the growing howls of the wind.

Ignoring him, Lilly shouted, "What can we do?"

"The HOG is the best chance you have," Chuck answered.

"*We* have," Mavid corrected.

He and Chuck looked at one another, having a conversation between themselves without words, ending with them both exchanging a nod.

"Mavid!" Jake yelled, pointing.

He raised the gun just in time to shoot the jaw off an approaching zombie, following up with a second shot that took the top of its skull off, exposing a still juicy brain that hadn't completely dried out.

The force of the wind picked up, making the three of them grab onto the HOG.

"We need to get this unstuck and I can take care of all of them!" Chuck hollered.

"What the fuck can we do?" Lilly yelled back.

Chuck shrugged and Mavid popped off three more shots, dropping another body to the ground. Jake looked back through the trees where they'd seen the funnel forming and saw it was moving down the hill toward them.

"It's about to get real bad!"

Lilly looked and saw what he was talking about. The tall trees around L.T.'s property were swaying as larger branches sheared off from the trunks and went flying. The tornado was gaining ground, chewing up everything in its path.

Chuck and Mavid finally saw the source of terror in the other two; a vicious twister was bearing down on them and they had nowhere to go.

Jake saw Lilly starting to slip as the tornado's suction intensified. He grabbed her arm and pulled with all his strength, helping her gain a sturdier hold. A few reanimated corpses flew past them. Mavid shone his light just in time to see them being ripped apart by the sheer force of the wind.

"We're fucked," yelled Lilly.

Feeling his legs being pulled out from under him, Jake dropped the flashlight and used both hands to keep himself anchored to the large HOG.

"Climb up and hold on!" Chuck yelled to the three of them before pulling the door shut to the cab and falling back into the seat.

Jake motioned with his head for Lilly to come on. Pulling themselves to the front of the machine, both risked being swept away as they helped Mavid up onto the boom arms. Lilly was next, Jake pushing from behind while she kept hold of whatever she could wrap her hands around. Jake was last to climb aboard, settling against the front of the cab as another group of zombies flew by, destined for certain death at the hands of the ungodly twister.

Handholds were scarce on the front of the machine, but Mavid, Jake, Lilly were doing their best. Chuck revved the engine and attempted to lift the entangled cutter, tires spinning in reverse. The tornado was helping, pulling the HOG away from the overturned F-150 until it finally unhooked whatever it was stuck on, shooting backward.

Jake planted his heels onto the boom arms and threw his arms out to prevent Mavid and Lilly from tumbling forward. Chuck shifted the transmission into drive and was now fighting to gain ground in the other direction, away from the deadly cyclone.

The cab provided enough cover from the sucking wind that Jake was able to ease his hold on the other two. Chuck raised the cutter blades as he pressed on toward the house and engaged them, sending a shower of sparks from metal grinding against metal off in all directions.

To Jake, all of the corpses seemed disoriented by everything that was going on. Before, they seemed to be driven to the living—and for whatever reason, L.T.'s house—but now, between the loud screeching of the HOG, and the wailing of the tornado, it seemed to be overloading whatever sensory receptors they still possessed.

Angry shrieks, dulled by loud, howling gusts, preceded the four of them as one by one, once-alive residents of Lordsland were chopped, bit by bit, and sent hurling into the air to feed the ever-growing funnel. The three outside the cab had to throw up their arms and shield themselves from the biological debris.

More and more dead folks walked headlong into the spinning blades of the HOG as Chuck brought them closer to the house, fighting against the tornado for every inch. Jake considered leaping off and making a mad dash for the door, but he couldn't leave Mavid and Lilly to fend for themselves.

Trying to talk was useless with the cacophony of noise surrounding them, so Jake grabbed one of each of the other's hands until he had their attention and inclined his head toward the house. They understood what he was trying to convey and nodded their heads.

Jake rose to a squatted position, and Lilly did the same. Mavid grabbed his arm and when Jake looked, the old man was mouthing something but he couldn't make out the words. Mavid tilted his head toward the cab and he looked.

"Chuck, right. Fuck," Jake uttered into the wind.

Looking back into the cab, he and Chuck locked eyes and he saw the farmer shake his head, as if reading his mind. Looking over the cab, Jake had to squint from all the flying particles in the air, but saw the tornado was now where the big military truck used to be. He turned and looked Mavid in the eyes, his face void of emotion, and shook his head. Mavid's eyes narrowed with thought and then the old man bowed his head forward slightly.

Turning forward, Jake saw a clear path to the front door and pointed for the other two to see. Readying himself to leap from the machine, he tapped Lilly on the leg and motioned for her to go.

He watched as she sprang forward, launching off the machine with grace. Moving over to where she had been, he counted down from three in his head and jumped.

Jake tried to hit the ground running, but his knees buckled and he went skidding across the gravel and leaves. Lilly was pulling him up before he could gather his wits.

"You fucked that one all to hell," she yelled.

On his feet, he spun around, expecting to see Mavid following suit. The HOG was turning away from the house, Mavid still riding on the front, his fists punching the air as Chuck continued forward toward the ripping whirlwind of horror.

"No!" Jake screamed and started to run after them.

Lilly grabbed him from behind and pulled him back toward the door. The two of them watched as the machine surged ahead, its cutting apparatus raised high, the headlights barely cutting through the outside layer of spinning debris.

A terrible groan filled the night—the sound of stubborn metal resisting the force of nature that would see it mangled beyond recognition. In the blink of an eye, the HOG was plucked from the ground like a toy and thrown into a nearby oak tree, first crumpling, then tearing apart and consumed by the tornado.

Not noticing the door open behind them, Jake and Lilly were pulled into the house.

Chapter Thirteen

Marie slammed the door shut as Jake stumbled into the living room. Alex rushed to him and threw his arms around his dad, squeezing him tighter than he ever had before. Lilly never stopped, walking straight down the hallway, disappearing from view.

"Holy shit, I think that thing is heading straight for us!" Spike yelled.

Christina rose from the couch, wobbling where she stood, clutching her side. "Get away from the window, you little shit. Don't you know not to stand by one during a storm?"

Spike rolled his eyes and waved her off, turning back to look outside. Don strode across the living room and grabbed Spike's arm. "She's right, it's too dangerous," he told the boy.

"You're not the boss of m—"

Spike's words were cut off when the sound of glass shattering filled the living room. Two grunts quickly followed and then everyone started to scream as gusts of wind blew into the house.

Jake looked on in disbelief of what he was seeing. A tree limb had darted in through the window and lanced through both Spike and Don. The sturdy branch pierced in and out of Spike's neck, and continued on into Don's heart.

Rachel, Marie, and Alex all reacted in the same manner and whimpered before shielding themselves from the gruesome scene. Christina cursed loudly, while Doc Butler rushed to the human kabob to assess the situation.

Jake knew they were already gone, but were held upright by the limb counterbalancing on the window sill. Butler looked up from the pair at Jake and shook his head before backing away from the two of them.

Don and Spike's bodies started to shake and then were pulled against the wall, a loud, sickening, wet pop ringing out over the wind as the branch was jerked from their bodies and sucked back into the storm.

"Jesus fucking Christ," Lilly said as she re-entered the living room just in time to see it all play out.

Jake's head snapped around to look at her at the exact moment the cuckoo clock fell from the wall, crashing to the floor, sounding out one last chime.

As Lilly came to her senses, their eyes met and then she said, "Everyone needs to come with me. NOW!" before turning to head back down the hallway.

Jake instructed Marie to take Alex and Rachel and go, shoving them all forward as they murmured amongst themselves. He then pulled Doc Butler across the living room and told him to follow the others. Finally, he turned to Christina—who gave him an odd look of surprise.

"You should've just left me on the couch. I'm too much of a bitch for anything to happen to me," she said as Jake wrapped her arm around his shoulders and helped her along.

He couldn't help but smile at her while moving down the hall. "Even so, that storm out there is one helluva motherfucker."

He felt her head nodding. "Been known to be a motherfucker a time or two in my day. People are kinky hoes."

Snickering as the wind at their back pushed them along, Jake saw everyone had gone into the master bedroom at the end of the hallway. He helped Christina into the room just as Butler's head disappeared beneath the floor, striking Jake as odd before remembering the others mentioning L.T. was a prepper.

"Bunker?" he asked Lilly.

"Bunker," she confirmed.

Peering into the hole, Jake saw Butler as he reached the bottom and disappeared from view. He had no doubt L.T. had gone all out for his doomsday fallback plan.

Prodding Christina along, he said, "You next, then Lilly."

For the first time since meeting the foul-mouthed woman, she didn't have anything quippy to say, or some smartass remark; the woman simply followed along. Getting her started on the ladder, Jake and Lilly each held one of the woman's arms until she was far enough down to grip the rungs—a cry of pain coming from her mouth with every movement.

Jake was about to tell Lilly she was next when a loud groan filled the house and then, as if all sound was muted from existence for the briefest of moments, the house seemed to inhale before the shattering of wood, glass, and everything else in the front half blasted their eardrums.

The diametrically opposed forces of pull and push grabbed hold of them, throwing them off kilter. Jake braced himself in the doorway and looked down the hallway to see the beating heart of the tornado that was determined to claim them all.

"GO! NOW!" he yelled as he turned, but saw she'd already had the same thought.

As Lilly disappeared from view, he pushed himself away from the doorframe, the push and pull sensation gave him the feeling of wading through molasses, and he had to fight for every step he took. In the final few feet, he threw himself at the hatch as the air around him became a high-powered vacuum. The metal portal was hard to hold on to, and he felt his grip slipping away. Panic flooded him and he closed his eyes, hoping Marie and Alex would survive after he was gone.

Just as his fingers released, he felt a hand grab his wrist and opened his eyes and looked. Lilly was there, scowling at him.

"Would you quit fucking around and get your ass in here!" she hollered.

Jake blinked once. "Okay."

Stilling his resolve, he gritted his teeth and pulled toward Lilly. The roaring wind ripped at his back as Jake moved away from encroaching death, into the arms of safety. Giving it everything he had, he used one last burst of energy to pull himself forward, into the hatch.

Lilly kept a hand on him until she knew he was safe. "Pull the lid closed!"

Jake stepped up one rung and found the heavy, hinged hatch sitting on the floor as more of the house was consumed by the hellacious twister. He struggled to lift it at first, but once he had it off the floor, he brought it down overhead with a loud thunk, and a jarring silence filled the bunker.

Twisting the locking mechanism in place, he descended the ladder and looked around the space at the stockpile of survival supplies, food, and weapons. The others all fanned out and sat wherever they'd found a spot, sitting in silence.

Jake found Marie, Alex, and Rachel sitting together on a cot in the corner and went to them. For the second time in twenty-four hours, the Wards—with the addition of Alex's classmate—huddled together and waited for the storm to pass.

Doc Butler told the group it was well past sunrise while looking at his wristwatch, and that the storm should be over. Lilly was first to her feet, nearly running to the ladder before starting to climb. Christina said she was completely content with staying put—after finding L. T.'s stash of liquor—and remained lounged out on the floor, taking another swig from the second bottle she'd cracked open.

Butler groaned as he stood and stretched, shaking off the lingering effects of nodding off in an odd position. He looked toward the cot and saw Jake was the only one that was awake. He and Butler exchanged a look of appreciation, the doc offering a crooked smile. Without an exchange of words, Butler left them and walked to the ladder.

Jake heard a squeal then a loud thunk and the area under the ladder lit up like a spotlight from overhead had been turned on. *Sunlight*, he thought and shifted on the cot, his heart more overjoyed to see the rays of light than it ever had before.

Looking down, his family, and Rachel, were all asleep, each one leaning on the other like fallen dominos. Jake reached around and started to rub Marie's shoulder, his attempt to wake her as gently as possible. Her eyes fluttered open and she looked up at him, a smile tracing over her lips.

"I think it's over," he said, barely above a whisper.

Marie stirred and inadvertently woke the two kids.

"What is it? Are we safe?" Rachel asked, already sitting up and looking around, wide-eyed.

"Shh, shh," Marie cooed, patting her on the back. "Everything is okay."

Alex rose and yawned loudly. "I gotta pee."

Jake and Marie laughed in unison, while Rachel wrinkled her nose.

"Yeah, I think I do, too, buddy. Let's go up and see where the others went."

At the ladder, before climbing, Jake looked up and saw nothing but clear sky above. A chill rippled over his skin as he thought about what that meant. One by one, he helped the others up until they were clear of the bunker. After another attempt of trying to encourage Christina to come with them, he left her to her own devices as she started to hum a tune to herself.

Jake climbed and left the bunker behind, standing in awe of the complete destruction the tornado had brought. Nothing filled the vast—now open—space where L.T.'s compound used to be. No debris, no trees, none of the vehicles, none of the dead bodies that had magically sprang to life yesterday... nothing, aside from the foundation of the house, and the lid of the shelter that had kept them all safe.

Off in the distance, Jake saw Doc Butler walking around, pausing here and there to look at something, then continued on while shaking his head. Farther off was Lilly, who was frantically jogging between different spots, as if searching for something—or someone.

As his son finished relieving himself, Alex and Rachel walked off together, conversing about something Jake couldn't hear.

As he stepped beside his wife, Marie looked at him.

"This is..."

"...a disaster," Jake finished for her.

She scoffed. "To put it lightly. Do you think it took our house as well?"

Wrapping his arm around her, Jake drew her into a hug. "I guess we'll find out. And if it did, we'll find another one somewhere else. Way the fuck away from here."

They both shared a laugh, but were cut short when Lilly screamed out. The two of them turned to look at what was going on.

Marie said, "Holy fuck!"

"Yeah..."

Watching as Lilly took off running down the driveway, they saw L.T. and Cici walking toward them. Never stopping, the bartender crashed into the man, driving him to the ground, planting kisses all over his haggard looking face.

Cici ran forward until catching up with Alex and Rachel, the dog's little tail wagging as the girl picked her up and snuggled her.

"I guess she's glad to see him?" Marie asked.

"Guess so. I wonder how the hell they managed to stay alive, though? Both of them..."

Taking a step back, Marie looked at Jake. "I guess you've got one hell of a story to write about now, dontcha?"

Grinning, Jake nodded before pulling her back into a hug. "For sure. You can't make this kind of shit up," he answered, sealing it with a kiss.

Paul sat up in the prison cell and looked around. He'd been dreaming about the time he and Renee Prickett snuck into the movie theater to watch Basic Instinct after all his friends at school told him there was nudity in it. Whether there was or not, Paul couldn't say, but he didn't care since it was the first time a girl let him get all the way to third base, despite his repeated attempts to steal a homerun.

Now, realizing it was only a memory, disappointment clouded his face as he rubbed the back of his neck. The hard surface he'd been sleeping on had kinked up his muscles and he stood and rotated his shoulders, trying to work them out.

Then it dawned on him just where he was, having stayed here more times than he could count—Lordsland's finest, free accommodations for anyone causing a fuss in town. Taking his palms and rubbing his eyes, he looked around and jerked back slightly from the scene that lay beyond the bars of the cell.

Heaps of dead bodies covered the floor, and the main entrance to the left stood wide open. A flood of what had happened before he'd passed out filled his thoughts. *Clint... fuck!*

"Hey, anybody around?" Paul yelled as he stepped up to the locked door of the holding cell.

His nose finally caught up with his eyes and the smell of putrid flesh hit like a sledgehammer, causing him to dry heave toward the floor.

Through watery eyes, Paul saw something shiny sitting on the dull, chipped, concrete floor. Raising his shirt to cover his nose, his body odor worked well to mask the stench of the dead, and he held onto the bars as he reached to retrieve whatever was by his feet.

Cold steel greeted his hand and he knew exactly what it was. Raising the snub nosed pistol close to his face, he released the cylinder and there was still one unspent shell in the gun. Ejecting the empty casings, he slapped the cylinder back into the frame and lowered the gun.

"Someone there?" he hollered through the fabric of his shirt.

Spinning the gun around in his hand, he used the butt end to bang on the bars, trying to create as much racket as he could in hopes of drawing someone's attention.

His stomach grumbled and he realized he hadn't eaten anything for at least a day. Turning away from the door, Paul searched the cell from top to bottom and didn't find anything of use.

Putting the gun in his pocket, he stepped over to the toilet-sink combo and lapped up water from his hands before taking a much needed piss.

Hours passed and his hunger grew cruel, the thick smell of decay battling with gnawing pain in his gut. His pleas for help had all gone unanswered, with no signs of life to be seen or heard from beyond the open door.

Paul took to pacing the length of the cell, trying to think of what to do, how he might unfuck the predicament he woke to find himself in. Every time he thought he'd figured out something ingenious, it ended in failure and he was back to square one.

The sunlight was starting to fade, casting long shadows across the street. He could see outside through the small sliver of freedom sitting mere feet away from his cell.

Begrudgingly laying down on the hard cot, Paul closed his eyes and hoped someone would come through the area tomorrow and free him.

A loud explosion from somewhere close by in the middle of the night startled him awake, and he fumbled around for the pistol in the dark, finally finding it next to where the cot was bolted to the wall.

"Who is it? Who's there?" Paul asked, his voice cracking as he aimed blindly at nothing.

He moved to the set of bars and strained his eyes for any movement.

"HELP! I'm alive in here!" he screamed

Nothing but silence—not even the sound of bugs from outside made any noise.

Paul began pacing back and forth in the cell again, but after the third time of bashing his shin on the lip of the toilet, he kicked it as hard as he could and sat on the cot.

"All I need is a fucking key!"

Sitting the gun next to him on the cot, Paul buried his face in his hands and stayed that way for the remainder of the night. Staying in the position for so long brought on a whole different set of aches when he woke, his legs numb from the thighs down.

Locking his knees, Paul had to brace himself against the wall until the circulation returned to his legs. After drinking a few handfuls of water, he went and stood at the bars and stared toward the street, praying to see someone pass by.

With endless hours of waiting for a miracle to fall into his lap, Paul had a lot of time to reflect. To think about how he treated the folks around him—particularly Clint. He'd never flat-out told the man he was his best friend, but that's the way he'd always seen him, and why he was always on his case and giving him a hard time.

"Tough love," his dad and uncles would tell Paul when he was growing up, always busting his balls about something.

And that's exactly what he was, a ball breaker, through and through—the perfect product of his environment.

Cramps stabbed him in the stomach, causing Paul to double over. He abandoned his post at the front of the cell and wobbled over where he fell onto the cot with a heavy thud.

"Fuck! Ouch!" he yelled, something digging into his back.

Reaching behind him, he pulled out the unforgiving steel that was the revolver and stared at it.

Looks mighty tasty, dunnit? The thought came out of nowhere, but he licked his lips as he looked into the muzzle. A memory surface of a guy he and Clint had run around with a few years back. Paul couldn't quite recall his name, but he did remember why the man wasn't around anymore.

"Russian roulette," he said aloud to the dead rotting away on the floor.

Popping the cylinder open, he looked at the single round and couldn't shake the thought from his head. Taking his hand and spinning the cylinder, he turned his hand quickly, locking it back into the frame. Opening his mouth, Paul pointed the gun at the roof of his mouth, his hand shaking, rattling the steel against his teeth.

"Fu— —is —hi—" he choked out around the gun and pulled the trigger.

Click.

Paul's head fell back against the cot and he began sobbing into the stained fabric of the flat pillow. By the time the sun had gone to bed, and the moon was giving off just enough light to make out loose shapes in the darkness, he sat up on the cot.

If asked what the emotion he was feeling was called, never in a million years could he have told you, but apathy filled him to the core. He was going to starve to death locked away in here, but... he didn't *have* to.

Repeating the process of releasing and spinning the cylinder, then slapping it back home, Paul put the gun back in his mouth—his hand steadier this time—and pulled the trigger.

Click.

"Two," he uttered before going through the steps again.

Click.

"Three."

As the moon gave way to the sun, another click was heard from the cell.

"Two-forty."

...

Click.
"Two-forty-one."

...

A shot rang out and then the clink of steel falling onto concrete sounded from within the police station.

"What the fuck was that?" someone asked from the street just outside.

The End

Epilogue

T he clacking from the keyboard stopped and Jake splayed his fingers out, relaxing the tension that was turning them into claws. He stared at the computer screen, re-reading the words "The End" and couldn't believe he'd pounded out an entire book in such a short span of time.

Shifting his head from one shoulder to the other, his neck popped and cracked and he felt as if a heavy weight had been lifted from his back.

The front door opened and Jake heard the lawn guy somewhere outside, pretending to blow leaves around, when the sound was cut off.

"Hey, hon. How was your morning?" Marie asked, walking into the living room where he was sitting on the couch.

Jake craned his head back, resting it against the couch, waiting for a kiss. "Not bad, actually. I just finished."

Marie planted a peck on his lips before looking over at his laptop screen. "'The end', did you finish the whole thing?" The surprise in her voice was noted by Jake.

"Is that so hard to believe? I'm a writer, you know?" He reached up and pulled her over the couch and started tickling her.

After leaving her lying upside down on the cushions—breathless—Jake got to his feet and walked toward the kitchen. "I need a cup of coffee."

As he set the pot to brew, he lowered the blinds with his finger and looked out at their backyard. "Oh shit," he said with a heavy sigh.

"What is it?" Marie asked, correcting herself to an upright position.

Jake turned to face her, his face growing long. "Looks like that storm last night blew a bunch of our stuff into Don's yard. I can see him out there talking to himself."

Marie pinched the bridge of her nose and sank low on the couch. The coffee pot gurgled as the drops fell into the pot. As he was pulling out a mug from the cupboard, Marie cleared her throat loudly and Jake retrieved another one to go along with his own.

Carrying the two steaming cups into the living room, he handed one down to his wife and took a sip from his and smacked his lips. "Not only am I good lay, but I brew one mean cup of Joe, if I do say so myself."

Marie nearly baptized him with the hot liquid in her mouth but was able to remain composed enough to swallow. "Dead Lord, help me with this one," she groaned and rolled her eyes.

Closing his eyes as he took another sip, Jake relished the semi-bitter dose of caffeine. "I better get out there and clean up the yard before Don gets Shipley down here to arrest me for littering."

Marie winked at him and rubbed his leg with her foot. She motioned with her head toward the laptop. "May I?"

He smiled. "You may."

Putting on his shoes, Jake left his wife to her reading and walked outside where the sunlight made him squint. Before his eyes could adjust and he could look around, Don had already spotted him and was yelling something unintelligible.

"Morning, Don," Jake said, keeping his tone neutral.

"This is a catastrophe, Ward!" Don proclaimed, standing with his hands on his hips at the very edge of his property.

"What's that, Don?"

"This... this! Don't you see it. All your crap had migrated over to my place." The distraught man began pacing, shaking his head and mumbling something too low for Jake to hear.

Keeping the laugh that was building in his chest bottled away, Jake stepped off his deck and looked around. "No sweat, Don. I'll have it all cleaned up in a jiff."

Don stopped on a dime and stared at his neighbor, a manic look of disgust and apathy in his eyes. Without a word, he walked away from Jake, slamming the door as he went back into his house.

As he walked across the space between their two properties, Jake looked toward his front yard and saw the lawn guy, *Ethan?* he pondered, trying to remember his name, walking around one of their Japanese Maple trees in circles. When he spotted Jake staring at him, he raised a hand in acknowledgment.

"Yeah, keep dicking around, asshat," Jake said as he waved back.

After an hour and a half of toting all his family's belongings back to their backyard—and catching Don hawking over him more than once—Jake was finally done and headed back inside.

A thin sheen of sweat coated his body, causing his clothes to stick to his skin. Peeling off his shirt, he said, "I'm going to take a quick shower."

Marie waved her hand absentmindedly in the air, too engrossed in his manuscript to reply properly.

Watching for a moment, seeing her face change from one reaction to another, he wondered what part she was at.

After toweling off and changing into some fresh clothes, he walked to the living room and stopped dead in his tracks. Marie glared at him from the couch.

"Ethan? You really think I'd be fucking around with... Ethan?!" she asked, menace in her voice.

Jake smiled to himself internally to have had the guy's name right. "It's just a story. Gees."

Walking over to the couch, he sat down next to his wife and took the laptop from her and looked at the screen. "Well, what'd you think?"

Looking over at her, Marie's eyes danced around the room as she thought about it. "It was interesting. There was a lot of gross stuff in there."

Jake looked back at the computer screen. "Yeah..."

"And poor Don! How could you?" She feigned shock in a dramatic fashion.

The two of them shared a laugh.

"So... Do you think it's worth keeping?" Jake asked, apprehension thick in his voice.

Marie got up from the couch and walked into the kitchen and started searching through the refrigerator and cabinets to figure out what they would have for dinner. "I don't know. It is *just* another zombie book, I guess. Up to you."

Jake nodded silently. He rubbed his fingertips over the keyboard, thinking hard about the story that had poured out of him that morning.

"Hey you, come help me pick something before you go to pick up Alex," Marie called.

Jake pressed the ctrl-A buttons together, highlighting all the text of the manuscript. His eyes lingered on the delete button, lost in deep thought.

"Hmm." The sound escaped his throat as he thought about it some more.

Moving the cursor off of the text, he moved it up to the corner and hit save, thinking at the very least, he'd trunk it for a rainy day.

Closing the laptop, Jake said, "Coming," and set the computer aside.

"Say," Marie started, "what was the name of that story, anyway?"

Jake thought for a moment, wondering if he had actually given it a title. Off the cuff, he said, "Deadly Grave Things!"

As he looked at his wife to see her reaction, Marie scrunched up her face and grimaced before going back to what she had been doing. "Not good?" he asked.

"Better go pick up Alex," she replied, quickly changing the subject.

Jake laughed. "Yeah. Be back in a bit, that is... if the Deadly Grave Things don't get me!" he said as he ran out the door like he was being chased.

The End...?

About the Author

From 100 word drabbles, to full-length novels, RJ Roles is an author that takes pride in his various works of horror fiction. He is the founder and admin of the Books of Horror Facebook group, and founder of From the Ashes. His stories span the the entire horror genre, as well as its sub-genres, and his pen often dips into many inkwells, creating unique, boundary crossing tales. He lives a quiet life with his wife and many cats in southern West Virginia. Find him on his website www.rjroles.com

Also By RJ Roles

Interested in more? Scan with your phone below.

www.ingramcontent.com/pod-product-compliance
Lightning Source LLC
Chambersburg PA
CBHW051425130726
47987CB00005B/1915